GOOD BONES

KIM FIELDING

Dreamspinner Press

Published by
Dreamspinner Press
382 NE 191st Street #88329
Miami, FL 33179-3899, USA
http://www.dreamspinnerpress.com/

Good Bones

Cover by Christine Griffin
alizarin_griffin@yahoo.com
http://christinegriffin.artworkfolio.com/

ISBN: 978-1-61372-485-9

Printed in the United States of America
First Edition
April 2012

eBook edition available
eBook ISBN: 978-1-61372-486-6

CHAPTER 1

DYLAN knew right after lunch that today he'd be cutting it close. The day leading up to the full moon was not a time to have everything else go wrong. But already a meeting had run much longer than scheduled. A client was being difficult. The budget was tight. Blueprints had to be adjusted. Tempers were frayed. As a result, it was well past four o'clock when he finally escaped the architectural firm. He mumbled an excuse to the secretary about an art show opening as he fled out the door and into another of Portland's overcast afternoons.

The situation still might have been under control, but Dylan made a stupid mistake, choosing the Hawthorne Bridge instead of the Marquam. Just as he came to the bridge, its red lights began flashing, and traffic stopped. He watched the center span rise at a glacial pace. The waiting cars were too tightly packed for Dylan to back up and take another route, so he waited, not listening to whatever was on National Public Radio, his fingers drumming impatiently on the steering wheel. He couldn't see what sort of vessel was passing under the bridge or why the hell it was taking so long.

In the Chevy next to him, the driver was using one finger to carefully excavate his nose. Dylan's windshield wipers swiped back and forth, *swish-squeak, swish-squeak*, each movement counting off more of his dwindling time. He took slow, deep breaths to quell his racing heart and jumpy nerves.

When he finally reached the other side of the river, Dylan was certain the sky was beginning to darken a little, although it was hard to tell for certain through the everlasting gloom of the clouds.

Fortunately, traffic on the west side was a bit lighter than usual, and Dylan drove as fast as he could, swerving around a bicyclist, running a light just changed to red, making pedestrians scowl. And then, just before he turned onto Jefferson, he got stuck behind a lumbering city bus with a seemingly narcoleptic driver. For several slow blocks, Dylan glared at the roaring tiger and trumpeting elephant emblazoned across the rear of the bus, but ultimately, he felt a certain sympathy for the wild denizens of the Oregon Zoo.

By the time he finally merged onto the freeway, the evening commute had begun in earnest, and traffic was crawling. Dylan tailgated and lane-switched and swore under his breath. His jaw ached, and his back was itching as if he were wearing a fur coat inside out. He gripped the steering wheel so tightly the plastic nearly cracked.

And then he came upon an accident. It wasn't a bad one—just an ordinary fender bender. A tow truck had already arrived, and several people were standing there in the drizzle talking on cell phones. Both of the vehicles involved had managed to pull onto the narrow shoulder, so traffic should have been able to pass unimpeded. But everyone slowed down to gawk as if they had never seen such an amazing sight, so all three lanes were stop and go. And stop. And go.

Dylan's nerves thrummed, and his skin felt too tight.

The one small grace was that his exit lane was open, so he shot down the off-ramp and zipped down the last mile of surface streets, silently praying that there were no police nearby, that no more impediments would appear. That he would make it on time. There was no question at all now; based on both his dashboard clock and the darkening sky, the sun was nearly set.

He parked his Prius in the driveway with a screech of brakes and ran for the front door. As he fumbled with the lock, his hand shook so wildly that he dropped the keys. *No, no, no,* a panicky part of his mind gibbered as he swooped up the keys and managed to get into the house. His bones were beginning to reshape themselves agonizingly, and his clothing was already ripping at the seams as he stumbled through the kitchen, down the hall, and into the spare bedroom. He growled through a lengthening jaw as he slammed the metal door closed.

Without fingers to remove the remains of his clothing, his last coherent human thought through the blinding pain was that he'd ruined yet another pair of Diesel jeans.

HE AWOKE as unpleasantly as always in the spare bedroom. He was naked, cold, and ravenous. He ached from sleeping on the hardwood floor. Ugly bruises had formed on his shoulders—he must have spent a good part of the night throwing himself against the door. Worst of all, though, was the emotion that seemed to pervade every molecule of his body. He didn't know a name for the feeling; maybe a name didn't exist. The closest he could come was *need* or *frustration*, but neither of those approached the intensity of what he felt. It was a little like being incredibly horny, only with no hope of ever getting laid again—a situation that was also unhappily familiar.

He stood and stretched and groaned, and he glared down at his incongruously perky cock. It was always much more optimistic than the rest of him. As usual, he decided to let it subside in favor of his bladder, which couldn't be ignored much longer. He resisted the urge to piss on one of the metal-sheathed walls and instead unfastened the complicated lock that he'd installed near the top of the door. The lock was too high for him to have reached during the night and too complex to be opened with teeth or claws. Opposable thumbs were handy things.

During his visit to the bathroom he couldn't help but catch sight of himself in the mirror. He looked as bad as he felt: hazel eyes bloodshot, skin pale, sandy curls in wild snarls. He considered calling in sick, but he'd done that last month and the month before, and he was worried that someone might notice a pattern. Nobody would be suspicious if a woman felt miserable every twenty-eight days, but people might wonder about a guy.

Fine. Shower it was. He shaved too, removing the dark-blond bristles from his cheeks and neatening the little patch on his chin. Then he brushed his teeth and tamed his hair and wandered into his bedroom to dress. His bed was still made up neatly, of course, big and comfortable, covered in a cozy down duvet. It would have been a lot more comfortable than the hard floor of the spare room. He swallowed a sigh and pulled on briefs and Levis, a navy and yellow Decemberists tee, and a plaid button-down. Hooray for casual Friday, when the already loose dress code was abandoned. He wasn't sure he could have survived a shirt and tie today, when his skin felt too tight and his bones felt too loose.

His now standard breakfast no longer horrified him: a package of wine-cured bacon, raw from the plastic and sort of gummy in his mouth; a half dozen cage-free eggs cracked into an oversized mug; a triple espresso with a teaspoon of sugar stirred in. He had once been vegan.

He pulled on socks and boots and his favorite gray hoodie and drove through the drizzle to work.

He probably looked hungover, or maybe stoned. The secretary raised her eyebrows at him but didn't say anything. On the other hand, his office-mate, Matty, had no problem speaking her mind. "Wild night, Dylan?" she asked.

He had to suppress a desperate laugh. "Not really."

She was sitting at her desk, squinting through glasses at her computer screen. She had a big cardboard cup from Stumptown cradled in one palm, and Dylan's wolf-enhanced sense of smell registered the cranberry muffin she'd had for breakfast. Low-fat, no doubt. She wore her usual black blouse and gray cardigan, and although he couldn't see her lower half, he knew there would be black slacks—and red flats because it was Friday. She smiled at him. "Come on. Give a girl a thrill. Spill."

"Sorry, Matty," he said with a shake of his head. She assumed that his social life was a lot more exciting than it really was. "I stayed home. Really."

"You don't look like a guy who stayed home."

He held up a hand in a mock Boy Scout salute. "I solemnly swear I went straight home and didn't leave again until this morning, when I came straight to work. Um, after the Starbucks drive-through."

"Fine. You went straight home. With whom?"

"Just me. I know I look like hell today, but it's not because I had fun last night. I feel a little under the weather."

She gave him a skeptical look but then turned her attention back to her computer. Dylan sagged a little with relief and collapsed into his own chair.

It was hard to concentrate on work, but he tried. The Maywood Drive clients had decided they wanted five bedrooms instead of four, and that meant he had to make adjustments to the roofline and to the supports that would keep the house from toppling down the hill. He wasn't happy with the way the balcony was wrapping around the southwestern edge of the house. And he'd really hoped to build a deck around a couple of stately Douglas firs, but now he wasn't sure he was going to be able to pull that off without some pretty major adjustments.

He declined Matty's offer to join her for lunch. Instead, he grabbed a sandwich and chips from the little deli across the street and ate them at his desk.

At 4:12, as he was congratulating himself on almost getting through the day, his phone rang.

"Hey, Dyldo."

Dylan smiled at the nickname that had driven him crazy when he was younger. "Hey yourself, Dickhead." His brother preferred to be called Rick. Where was the fun in that?

"Dinner tonight."

"Thanks, but I think I'm gonna—"

"Wasn't an invitation, kid—it's an order. Seven o'clock, Hopworks."

Dylan knew better than to waste time arguing. "Fine," he sighed. "But is Kay gonna—"

"My better half will not be attending. Her sister's coming over, and they're going to make stuff for that craft fair they're doing next weekend. I think it involves putting mustaches on drinking glasses... or something nuts like that."

"Thus your dinner plans."

"That and other reasons," Rick said enigmatically. "Seven o'clock, Dyldo."

Before Dylan had a chance to mumble a reply, his brother had hung up.

There wasn't much point in driving all the way across town and then coming back, so Dylan stayed at the office, working on those plans. He waved at Matty when she left, refilled his mug from the coffeemaker in the corner, and by 6:40 he'd actually made some headway on the house.

The restaurant was crowded and noisy, but Rick had arrived early and snagged them a table, one of the tall ones with high seats. As soon as Dylan entered, Rick waved him over. Rick already had a plate of hummus and a pint of beer in front of him. "Organic IPA," he said as Dylan took his chair. "Want one?"

Dylan shook his head, then scooped some hummus onto a little pita triangle. With his mouth full he replied, "Stout. And meat. Lots of meat."

Rick's bushy eyebrows drew together in a frown. "I forgot. It's that time of the month again, isn't it?"

"Last night. I'm good now."

"You don't look so good, Dyldo."

"Fuck you."

The waitress appeared at that moment. She was tall and lean and muscular with stars tattooed on her bicep. "What can I get you?" she asked. He ordered his drink and a burger as rare as they could get it, while Rick made a face and asked for a chicken wrap and another IPA.

"Two beers?" said Dylan with a smirk. "Really living it up tonight, huh?"

"Shut up. When's the last time you went out with someone you weren't related to?"

"Fuck you," Dylan repeated.

Rick smiled and scooped hummus onto a pita. "I didn't actually invite you here to nag about your social life, though."

"Then why?"

A shrug. "Haven't seen you in a while. Wanted to know how it's going."

"'M all right. Work's busy. How about you and Kay?"

"Still trying on the baby thing." He took a long swallow of his beer. "She's got all these little charts. Man, it takes all the romance out of things when you gotta worry about ovulation cycles and the right position and all that shit."

"I wouldn't know," Dylan replied, not without sympathy. He knew how badly Rick wanted a kid.

"Yeah, well, if it doesn't work this month her doc says I gotta get tested. You know, jack off into a cup, see if the little swimmers know what the fuck they're doing."

"That sounds fun."

"Remember back in high school? When me and Jessica had that scare?" He shook his head slowly. "Who knew that fifteen years later I'd be rooting for the other side?"

The waitress appeared with Dylan's stout and Rick's refill. Dylan took a grateful sip.

"You had another close one, didn't you?"

Dylan didn't realize he'd closed his eyes until Rick asked the question, and then Dylan looked at him sharply. "I'm fine."

"No you're not."

"Look, Ricky...." That childhood name went way back, all the way to when Rick was Dylan's god: the Big Kid who rode a bike without training wheels and wore a Spider-Man backpack to school and didn't need a safety railing to keep him from tumbling out of bed at night. "It's under control, really. Yesterday was a fluke. The meeting went late, and the bridge was up and—"

"How many flukes, Dyl? In the last six months, how many times have you just barely made it?"

7

Dylan didn't answer. He looked away, over at the table next to them where a group of college students was laughing over a text message on someone's phone. And Rick didn't push it, so the brothers sat there drinking silently until the waitress came by with their dinners. Dylan's burger was good, and he was hungrier than he'd realized. Before he knew it, his plate was empty except for a piece of wilted lettuce. He looked up at Rick, who was still toying with a strip of tortilla.

"I don't know what you want me to do about it," Dylan said quietly. "It's not like I can hire a babysitter to make sure I'm locked up safely. Or... or a goddamn petsitter."

"Move in with us. We can rig something in the basement."

"Yeah? Are you really willing to trust me around Kay?"

"Kay knows the risks. She's willing."

Despite his despair, Dylan felt a touch of warmth for his sister-in-law. Poor thing didn't have a clue what she was marrying into a couple of years ago, but she'd loyally stuck around. Too loyal, maybe, because it didn't sound like she and Rick had thought through all the consequences. Dylan sighed. "And what happens when that baby finally appears?"

Rick winced a little and looked down at his plate. "That's not gonna be for a while yet."

"I know. But I'm not going to find a miraculous cure in the meantime."

"But you can't just go on like this, Dyl. Sooner or later you're gonna be just a little too late, and then...." He didn't finish his sentence, and he didn't have to. Dylan knew what his brother was thinking: *And then it's going to be like the first time.*

Dylan couldn't argue because he knew Rick was right. In fact, he knew if he ever screwed up again, it was going to be a hell of a lot worse than the first time, because now Dylan was stronger. Hungrier. He dropped his head into the palms of his hands and rubbed at his brows. "Maybe I should move to the wilderness. Alaska or something. Somewhere... far."

"You can't live by yourself."

"Well I can't fucking live with anyone else!" Dylan replied, louder than he'd intended. People nearby turned to stare for a moment before looking away again. They all had normal problems, like cheating boyfriends or crappy bosses or cars that kept breaking down.

Rick, bless his stubborn hide, didn't take offense. He knew that Dylan tended to react angrily when he was actually scared. "How would you even survive?" he asked reasonably. "I mean, I guess once a month you could, um, hunt. But what about the other twenty-seven days? Gonna take to designing igloos? I bet you'd make really cool ones. Green materials and energy efficient."

Dylan snorted a small laugh and even managed a smile when the waitress came to take their empty plates. He'd worked his way through school as a barista, and he knew how shitty it was when customers took out their hard days on their servers. When she went away, he said, "Maybe I could telecommute from the North Pole."

The grin left Rick's face; he was suddenly all serious. "Could you really do that? Telecommute, I mean?"

"Sort of. I could probably pull off going into the office, like, twice a week. For meetings and stuff. But I don't really see myself hopping on a plane from the Great White North twice a week."

"You don't have to!" Rick was bouncing up and down a little with excitement, so much like his younger self that Dylan had to smile. "There's plenty of boonies around here, Dyl. Get yourself a cabin in the Coast Range or something—that drive wouldn't be so bad a couple of times a week. Could you time it so you'd be out in the woods every twenty-eighth day?"

Dylan swallowed the last of his stout as he considered his brother's idea. He'd never been a back-to-nature type—they'd lived in the 'burbs when he was a kid, and he lived there now, albeit in a somewhat more stylish and expensive incarnation. He'd always thought it might be kind of cool to live right downtown, but that was… before. He spent a few minutes imagining himself loping through ferns and leaping over downed tree trunks, snuffling at the feast of scents, maybe finding a flat spot where he could finally run full out, his muscles bunching and flexing as he flew over the ground. And then leaping, feeling his powerful jaws clamp down as hot blood filled his mouth—

He looked up at his brother guiltily, feeling absurdly like he'd been thinking about sex. "That's an interesting idea, Dickhead."

Rick grinned hugely. "I guess big brother's still got it, Dyldo."

The waitress came by with their bill, and Rick pointed her in Dylan's direction. "My little brother's got it."

Dylan pulled out his wallet good-naturedly. "Is that all this was? A way to scrounge a free meal?"

"You owe me."

As Dylan counted out the cash, Rick slid off his stool and stretched a little. "I'm gonna head home, see if the little woman needs some help with her mustaches."

DYLAN was always restless for a night or two after he changed, so knowing he wouldn't sleep anyway, he decided he might as well get some work done. On the way home from Hopworks he did a drive-through for a Venti latte with a quad shot of espresso. It was still hot enough to burn his tongue when he walked into his house. He set the coffee and laptop on the kitchen table and went into the bedroom to undress.

The house was as neat as always. The reinforced door to the spare bedroom was, as usual, tightly closed so the shredded clothes and new claw marks on the walls were safely hidden. He'd need to go in and clean in a day or two. In his bedroom, everything was in place. He always made sure of that on the day before he changed, as if having a couple of throw pillows on the bed and the dresser thoroughly dusted would help remind him that he was human and civilized. He liked to think that his bedroom—and most of the rest of the house, for that matter—looked like a magazine spread. *Dwell*, maybe, or *Wallpaper*. But tonight it suddenly struck him that what his rooms actually resembled was a boutique hotel: attractive and sort of hip, but devoid of life.

With a touch of defiance, he kicked his shoes randomly across the bedroom floor and left his jeans and shirts in a heap near the door. It didn't help, though. Now it just looked like a slightly messy hotel room.

He tended to run hot this time of the month and padded back into the kitchen wearing only his low-rise briefs. He sat down at the table and sipped his coffee while his MacBook booted up.

He tried to answer a few e-mails from work and tweak his kitchen plans for the Maywood Drive project, but he couldn't focus. "Fine," he muttered to himself. He'd surf a few real estate sites instead. Maybe Rick's idea wasn't such a bad one.

Somehow, however, he found himself typing *gay.com* instead.

The photos varied: men in various states of undress posed in front of mirrors; men looking rugged beside waterfalls or atop boulders; men in suits and ties; men in plaid shirts, grinning, with their arms around their pals; men close up and smiling; men in black and white, striking models' poses. Men with muscles and men with pudge; bulky men in leather and fey boys with eyeliner; men with forests of dark fur on their chests and men whose skin was bare and oiled. Young men and old. Men who looked scary and men who looked like tax attorneys. Handsome men. Plain men.

These men listed kinks aplenty: BDSM and cross-dressing and role-playing and spandex and exhibitionism and watersports and threesomes and medical play. There were some kinks Dylan had never heard of and a few others he hoped he'd never hear of again. But with all this variety—a rainbow of gayness—not a single man mentioned the one thing that mattered the most to Dylan: not one of them said a word about having a thing for werewolves.

His chest tight, Dylan slammed the laptop closed without shutting it down, ignored his cooled latte, and wandered into the living room to see if *House Hunters* was on.

CHAPTER 2

"YOU'RE gonna love this one!"

The Realtor's attempts at sounding positive and enthusiastic were becoming a little strained. Not surprising, considering that this was the tenth time they were driving way the hell into the middle of nowhere to view a property—the first nine tries had been complete failures. They had all been rural, but most had been nowhere near isolated enough for Dylan's needs. They had looked at one place that had no neighbors for miles, but it turned out to be a falling-down shack halfway up the mountain, on a road that would be impassible part of the year, with no cell phone signal and no power supply other than a generator.

Dylan squirmed a little in his seat and grunted in reply. Matty had recommended Steve Nguyen, but it turned out that Steve usually specialized in high-rise condos and knew almost nothing about country living. Considering Steve's bold attempts at flirting, Dylan suspected that Matty had something other than property acquisition in mind when she hooked them up. Dylan was going to have a little chat with her about how much he didn't need a matchmaker.

But for now, he was stuck in a Honda Civic with Steve, a good hour from anything resembling civilization, with Steve looking at him nervously, as if he wasn't sure whether to kiss Dylan or boot him out of the car. Dylan had turned slightly sullen after the seventh or eighth unproductive viewing.

Steve had already turned off the main highway onto a state road that twisted through farmland and trees, and now he turned onto gravel. "The county maintains this road, and the elevation is too low for snow," he chirped. The Civic bumped along, sending up little sprays of mud.

"How big is the property?" Dylan asked.

"Almost thirty acres. Most of it's too steep to grow anything, and there's a pond covering part of it. It was once a Christmas tree farm, but I guess that's all gone wild now."

"Neighbors?"

"Just one. And the land backs up to state forest."

That sounded promising at least, but Dylan didn't get his hopes up. They were bouncing past a long, empty field edged by a steeply rising wooded slope. No livestock were visible in the area, which was also a relief. Dylan wasn't at all sure he'd be able to resist the lure of beef on the hoof.

The road curved around a stand of firs, and Steve slowed to a halt. There were two houses there, with a long line of poplars between them. The sight of the house on the left got Dylan's pulse racing—it was a two-story farmhouse, maybe a century old, with porches on the first and second floors and green and brown trim against white wooden siding. The paint was peeling a little, and even from the car Dylan could tell the house needed some major work, but he liked the shape of it, the way the two chimneys rose confidently above the steep roof, the many large windows that were pleasingly arranged. But the other house made him scowl. It was a tiny place, probably dating from the '50s, and although most of it was hidden behind overgrown shrubs, the part he could see looked like it ought to be condemned.

"Tell me it's the two-story," Dylan said as they climbed out of the car.

"Yep! This was all one big farm, but a couple of generations back a pair of brothers had a falling out. One of 'em got the old house, and the other got all the usable land. I don't know why he built his house so close to the other. Convenient to the power lines, maybe. Or maybe just spite."

"Great. The old guys still live here?"

"No. Your house has been empty a while." They walked across the gravel toward the front porch. "I think a grandson's living in the other place."

"I was really hoping for no neighbors at all."

Steve huffed impatiently as he worked at unlocking the front door. "That's pretty hard to find, Dylan. Unless you want to really go back to nature. Come on. This is hardly an urban jungle here. Why are you being so antisocial, anyway?"

The Realtor had been trying for days to figure out why Dylan wanted to live in the sticks, and Dylan had given evasive answers about needing peace and quiet to work. Dylan wondered if Steve was starting to suspect that he was running a criminal enterprise of some kind. Growing pot, maybe. Or serial killing. Dylan made a face; that last guess wouldn't be so far from the truth.

But his mood lifted as they entered the house. Yeah, peeling wallpaper and hideous shag carpet, but the molding was original and miraculously unpainted, the ceilings were high, two of the rooms had huge fireplaces, and the windowpanes were slightly wavy old glass. The kitchen was cramped and a hideous mixture of '50s and '70s décor, but it would be easy to gut it and tear out the wall shared with the old dining room. That would still leave a living room downstairs, a bedroom he could convert to an office, and a half bath.

The upper floor had four bedrooms and two full baths. He'd probably combine two of the bedrooms into one and expand the master bathroom, and he'd have the enormous claw-foot tub re-surfaced. He could tuck in a window seat nicely along the south wall, where there was a view down a thickly overgrown hillside. The carpet was even more awful upstairs than down, but when he tugged a corner free, his suspicions were confirmed: decent hardwood underneath.

A narrow door in the hallway concealed a flight of stairs leading to the attic. Nothing up there but hints of mice and bats, barely any insulation at all, but there was no water damage, and the roof joists looked solid.

"Whaddaya think?" Steve asked, bouncing on the balls of his feet.

Dylan grunted noncommittally. "It's in pretty rough shape."

"Not really. Okay, yeah, it needs... cosmetic work. But it got rewired about ten years ago, and there's a new furnace." He patted a wall. "Good bones."

Dylan was already wondering how hard it would be to wolf-proof a bedroom or maybe install a solid cage somewhere. But he pretended to be skeptical, poking at the chimney bricks and peering at a windowsill. Then he turned back to Steve. "Let me see the heating and electrical."

Those turned out to be in the basement. It was a big basement, cool and dry, with another half bath tucked behind an area that must have once been a workshop. Tool shapes were still outlined on a wall-mounted pegboard. Another area was walled off and lined with shelves. It had probably once been used to store canned goods and the like, but with a heavily reinforced door it would serve pretty well as werewolf containment. There was even a tiny rectangle of window, too small and high for escape but adequate for a little welcome daylight the morning after.

The furnace needed cleaning but was otherwise in good shape, and the circuit breakers looked fine. The foundation looked solid too.

By the time they went outside to walk the property, Dylan's heart was racing with excitement. But he tried to play it cool, stepping slowly around a leafless blackberry bramble as they made their way down a narrow dirt path. Even this early in the season, wildflowers were beginning to bloom. Hawks circled overhead, dark against the gray sky, and a jay called hoarsely from the poplar stand.

Steve's spiffy shoes were getting muddy. "I guess you could bring in a Caterpillar and clear all this out," he said, waving his arms vaguely.

"Why bother? Not like I'm gonna grow veggies or anything." Dylan smiled evilly. "Besides, think of all the stuff you could hide in this jungle."

The Realtor gave him an uncertain look, then seemed to decide that Dylan was joking—probably. But it was Dylan who led them down the hill to a pond that had been formed by a low earthen dam. Most of the pond bank was crowded with trees and ferns and was pretty inaccessible to humans, but something low and four-legged could likely make its way down there, maybe to slink around in search of creatures who came for a drink.

Steve said, "It's big enough for a little boat, if you could get one down here. Kayak maybe."

"You think there's any fish?"

"Dunno. Maybe."

After several minutes, they hiked uphill to explore the rest of the property. It was hard to form a clear picture due to the uneven topography, but Dylan figured that the parcel was roughly pie-shaped, with the house at the pointy end near the road, forest along one side and at the back, and the poplars and brother's fields along the remaining side. The over-tall Christmas trees were there too, with the underbrush almost masking the evenly spaced rows.

"I wonder if there's much wildlife," Dylan said as nonchalantly as possible.

"Oh, I'm sure there is. Deer and coyotes for sure. Elk? I dunno—maybe even bears. And probably water things, like beavers or otters."

I wonder what beaver tastes like, Dylan thought, and barely managed to stifle a laugh. Maybe he made a funny face, though, because Steve gave him another worried look.

There were a few outbuildings to inspect: a newer structure that could be used as a garage or small barn, a small pump house for the well, and a half-collapsed chicken coop. Dylan nodded at them all and wondered whether it was annoying to eat through feathers.

"So whaddaya think?" Steve asked as they returned to the porch. He was grinning again, maybe because for once Dylan hadn't given him a flat-out no.

But Dylan scratched his neck thoughtfully. "I don't know. The house needs all that work, and it's more square footage than I need."

"Maybe you'll get a roommate one of these days," Steven replied with a slight eyebrow waggle.

"Doubt it."

Steve deflated only a little. It was clear that he smelled a commission in the air. "Well, close off the rooms you don't need. Or you could find uses for 'em. Home gym, maybe. Media room. Hobby room? Maybe a man cave."

Dylan rolled his eyes. "Who needs a man cave when he's got the whole place to himself?"

Another eyebrow waggle with a leer added in. "Playroom?"

Dylan snorted. The truth was he *wanted* this place, more than he'd wanted anything in a long time. But he'd also learned—in life and in love—that wanting led to disappointment, so he tried to dampen his own enthusiasm.

"You know what else?" Steve asked. "This place is a steal. The family just wants to get rid of it. They're tired of paying taxes on it, I guess. It's too far off the beaten path to turn into a B&B, land's no good for a hobby farm, and it's been on the market a while. They're asking four fifty, but I bet you could get it for under four."

That was within Dylan's budget, even figuring in the substantial amount he would have to put into remodeling the house. And he'd probably have to trade in the Prius for a pickup.

Up until this point he'd been considering the move to the country as a grim necessity, but it suddenly occurred to him that he might be happy out here—or some facsimile of happy. For the first time ever his blueprints would be for him. He could make his space personal, truly his. He could make it a home.

"I'm still not too sure about the neighbor," he said. "That house is pretty close."

"Yeah, but the trees are in between."

"What about in winter?"

"They're just starting to leaf out now, and you can barely see the place."

"But from upstairs?"

Steve sighed melodramatically. "Why don't you go up and take another look? I'll wait down here. I got a couple calls to make." He held up his Blackberry with a smile. "See? I even get four bars."

Dylan walked back up the stairs, noting some squeaking treads and a loose banister along the way. The stairs took a turn halfway up, and the landing was roomy enough for a nice built-in bookcase with glass doors.

The best view of the neighboring property was from the smallest bedroom, a space with faded yellow walls and a hideous flowery wallpaper border at chair-rail height. The large window was unencumbered by any kind of curtains, although there were small holes in the window frame where a rod had once been attached. Grubby fingerprints marred the paint next to the window, as if someone had spent a lot of time leaning there.

Now it was Dylan's turn to lean. Steve was right: even with the poplars barely leafed out, the branches obscured most of the house next door. But there was a gap in the trees—almost as if several of them had been removed—and through that space he could see the neighbor's back porch. Dylan recognized that he was using the term loosely. Unstained wood set on cinderblocks wasn't his usual definition of "porch." As far as he could tell, the primary outdoor décor consisted of piles of beer cans, rows of beer bottles, and two or three pots containing bare sticks that might once have been plants. There was also an ancient, warped metal-and-plastic lawn chair, a few buckets of unknown purpose, and an upturned wooden picnic table.

Nothing like a boutique hotel.

Dylan spent several minutes at the window, thinking about the risks. Steve was right—he wasn't going to find a home more isolated than this one, not unless he planned to cut his ties with the rest of the world. Although his social calendar was rather paltry, he wasn't ready to withdraw completely. If he bought this house a risk would remain. But hopefully the slob next door would be too drunk to venture outside at night.

Christ, he really, really wanted this house.

As he hovered uncertainly, his eyes caught a flash of movement. At first he thought it might be a bird or squirrel in the poplars, but then a human being came into view. A male human being—his gender pretty clear since he was wearing nothing but a tight green T-shirt. He had a cigarette in one hand. As Dylan watched, the man padded to the edge of the porch, stuck the cigarette in his mouth, took his dick in his other hand, and pissed into a thicket of weeds. He seemed to stand there forever, smoking and spraying, his eyes focused on nothing in particular.

And then, just as Dylan was becoming convinced the guy had a ten-gallon bladder, the man glanced up at Dylan's window. His mouth dropped open, and his cigarette tumbled to the ground. The last driblets of piss landed on his bare feet. He spun and marched back into the house. Dylan was too far away and at the wrong angle to be sure, but it looked like the neighbor had a spectacularly nice ass.

BY THE time Dylan returned to the Honda, Steve had finished his phone calls and was leaning against the driver's side door, staring off to the east. "I bet you can see Mount Hood from here on a clear day," Steve said.

"Terrific."

"So, what do you think?"

"It... it has potential."

An enormous grin lit up Steve's face. "I said you were gonna love this place!"

"I wouldn't call it love. But I guess I'm interested."

"Not even a crush?"

Dylan had to admit, Steve was kind of annoyingly adorable, like a golden retriever puppy who kept plopping a soggy tennis ball in your lap. "Maybe," he admitted.

Steve just about rubbed his hands in glee. He opened his mouth to say something—probably to ask what kind of offer Dylan would make—but then something behind Dylan caught his attention. Dylan turned to see the next-door neighbor approaching them.

He'd put pants on. Tight, faded jeans that emphasized his muscular build. At ground level Dylan had a much better view of the guy. He was probably a little short of thirty, with too-long dark hair falling over his square, handsome face. His skin was tan, and he had a sort of rolling gait like a cowboy. He didn't seem to be cold even though he wasn't wearing a jacket, and his feet were clad in ancient, holey sneakers. As he drew closer, Dylan saw that the man was a few inches shorter than his own shade-under-six-feet and that his eyes were a clear and startling blue.

"You scared the hell out of me," the man said by way of greeting.

"I was just looking at the house," replied Dylan with a frown.

But the man grinned. "I know. But for a second there I thought you were the old man." He pointed in the general direction of the window where Dylan had been standing. "He used to stand there for hours, just starin'."

"And that's why you wander outside naked?"

Steve goggled a little at that news, but the neighbor's smile didn't fade. "Old man's been dead for years, dude. I thought you were a ghost."

Wrong monster, Dylan thought.

There was a short, slightly awkward silence as the man and Dylan sized each other up. The man was no doubt taking in Dylan's soul patch and Art Not War T-shirt, while Dylan stared at the way the guy's John Deere tee stretched in interesting ways. The man's smile morphed into an amused smirk, and he stuck out a grease-stained hand. "Chris Nock."

"Dylan Warner," he replied, trying for as firm a handshake as possible.

"Bob or Thomas? I bet your parents are old-school hippies."

Dylan was a little surprised that Nock had heard of the poet. "My parents are dead."

The arrogant smile faded a little and Nock shrugged. "Sorry, dude. Mine too."

Dylan didn't think they were going to bond much over that, but in any case Steve chose that moment to position himself between them as if he were guarding Dylan. "Mr. Warner's considering purchasing this property," he said, sounding so prissy even Dylan rolled his eyes. "But he has some concerns over the proximity of your... place."

Nock's eyes stayed on Dylan. "You some kind of hipster hermit or something?"

"Something like that," Dylan replied.

"No problem. I'll stay out of your hair. I'll probably even keep my clothes on when I'm outside."

Dylan nodded slightly, hoping the guy didn't notice his flushed face.

Nock seemed to be waiting for another response, but when Dylan remained silent, the man shrugged again. "Well, good luck with it, man. It'd be nice to have someone living in the old heap, even if he'd rather play Peeping Tom than have a neighborly chat." He gave Dylan one more half smile, still ignoring Steve completely, then turned and walked back to his house.

"He doesn't seem too bad," Steve said when Nock was out of earshot. "Kind of rustic, maybe, but what do you expect out here?"

Dylan chewed on his lip for a while, looking at the vacant house. He could picture himself on the porch on a summer day. He'd have a bottle of beer near at hand, droplets condensing on the glass and rolling down, the Dandy Warhols or maybe even Pink Martini playing softly on his iPod, a set of brilliant architectural plans on his laptop. And he'd know that, even if he was due to change that night, he didn't have to worry about hurrying to his self-made prison. When the sun set he could simply shed his clothes and his human form and finally give in to the urges that had been gnawing at him for so long.

The Realtor must have been pretty practiced at his art, because he knew enough to keep his mouth shut while Dylan daydreamed. When Dylan finally opened the car door and folded into the passenger seat, Steve climbed behind the wheel. "So?" Steve asked.

"You think they'll go for three eighty-five?"

CHAPTER 3

"SO YOU'RE really serious about this thing," Matty said, stealing a french fry off Dylan's plate.

"I better be. We close next week, and I've already got a buyer lined up for my place in town."

She sat back in her seat with a frown. "I don't get it. I thought we made good roomies."

"I liked sharing an office with you, Matt. It's not you, it's me."

"Oh God. That's exactly what my last three boyfriends said when they dumped me. Is it in the Y-Chromosome User's Manual or something?"

He grinned. "On page five. But, you know, don't tell anyone I told you."

She rolled her eyes, and then they were both distracted as a hunk in an expensive suit brushed past their table. The guy turned and eyed Dylan briefly before moving on to the restaurant's exit, and Matty huffed melodramatically. "Jeez, Dylan. They practically throw themselves at your feet."

He pushed down his sudden longing and, focusing, took a bite of his cheesesteak sandwich.

"So come on," she said. "Why the change of scenery? I never really pictured you as the back-to-nature type." Dylan had to muffle a snort with another mouthful of food and hoped she'd drop the subject, but she speared a cherry tomato and then pointed her fork at him. "Spill."

"I just... I need something different. Some*where* different."
Which wasn't a lie, and if she assumed he needed peace and quiet to
court his muse or to get his head on straight, well, that wasn't his fault.
"It's not like I'm going to Mars or anything—I'll still be in the office
once a week."

"Won't be the same. They're probably gonna make me share with
Brian now."

Dylan smiled cruelly. "Then I hope you're ready to cultivate an
avid interest in the Trailblazers."

She made a momentary sour face but then pointed her fork again,
this time at a pair of forty-something men a few tables over. "And how
are you gonna meet anyone if you're spending all your time in Podunk?
They don't have gay bars in the wilderness."

"First off, meeting someone isn't my first priority. Second, get
with the times—they've been allowing queers in Podunk since 1994.
As long as we don't scare the livestock. And third, those two gentlemen
are straight."

"So you have perfectly honed gaydar."

"I do." He'd always had a pretty good idea of which men were
into men, even though until a couple of years ago very few of them had
been into him. Not until he met Andy. But that wasn't a line of thought
he wanted to pursue just then, so he finished off his sandwich and
snagged the last fry before Matty could get it.

"You know," Matty said, smiling slyly, "Steve thinks you're
pretty cute."

"Are we back in junior high now?"

She kicked at his shin. "He does."

"He's a nice guy. But he's not really my type, and anyway, I'm
not in the market. So please don't encourage him. Really, Matty. Life's
not all about people lined up in happy little pairs like... like Noah's ark.
I'm good, okay?"

"Fine. Just don't be a stranger."

He grinned at her. "No stranger than usual."

DYLAN'S furniture was more suited for an upscale contemporary home than a farmhouse, and it would only get in the way while he was renovating the new place, so he sold most of it on craigslist. He did keep a few things, though, like his bed and dresser and the budget drafting table he'd had since college. All it took was a single early-morning trip in a small rented U-Haul to schlep his stuff. Rick came along and helped him move in.

"I'm getting *old*," Rick said with a groan and a stretch after they'd set the mattress in place.

Dylan kicked a cardboard box full of clothing into the corner. "Well, I appreciate the help, old man."

Together they walked back through the house into the kitchen, where rooster wallpaper presided over cracked Formica and worn green vinyl flooring. "I'm gonna start in here," Dylan announced. "Gut it, knock down the wall, start from scratch. I'm thinking hickory cabinets, granite counters, a nice big island in the middle."

"Are you gonna turn all Martha Stewart on us, Dyldo?"

"Nah. Still going to eat a lot of frozen pizza. But I'll look stylish while I do."

Rick looked up at the stained ceiling, then over at a pile of mouse droppings where the refrigerator used to be. "It's not a solo job. You know guys willing to come all the way out here?"

Dylan had thought about that quite a bit, and it sort of worried him, but he didn't want to admit that. "I talked to a couple of contractors, but I'd rather do it myself. Those guys drag everything out, and they always go way over the estimates."

"Just don't expect me to be swinging hammers for you, kid. I've been working a lot of overtime lately, and Kay's still got my dick on call. Too bad the two of you can't synchronize your cycles or something."

Dylan flipped him the bird and Rick smirked, but then his face grew serious. "Have you rigged up any… containment yet?"

"Not yet. I have a few days to go, and it won't take long. Anyway, I think things are pretty safe out here."

"Okay. But the guy next door?"

"Haven't seen him. He probably spends his nights inside watching NASCAR."

They laughed, and Rick hugged Dylan. That would once have been overwhelming, because Rick was a big guy and Dylan used to be pretty scrawny. But he had put on a lot of mass since he was bitten. He didn't look like one of those overbuilt guys who spent their lives in the gym—he didn't even have the kind of impressive build that Chris Nock sported—but he was strong. One guy said he was built like a pro swimmer, and maybe it was just a creative pick-up line, but maybe not. In any case, when it came to competitive fraternal hugging, he could now give better than he got, and it was Rick who was left slightly breathless and rubbing his biceps.

On the return trip, Dylan took Rick home, and Kay greeted Dylan with a potted orchid and a batch of cupcakes. "Housewarming gifts!" she said and kissed his cheek. He ended up staying for lunch, then turned in the rental truck and bought a dorm-sized fridge at Costco to tide him over until the kitchen reno was complete. It was drizzling by the time he reached Scappoose, and he stopped at Fred Meyer for basic groceries, emergency candles, and a few other supplies.

By the time he finally parked in front of his new house, the mist had intensified to a shower. He ran his groceries inside, lugged in and set up the fridge, and put the cold stuff away. He was exhausted, sore, and a little overwhelmed by the size of the project that lay ahead of him, but he also felt more at peace than he had in ages.

He ended up eating three of Kay's cupcakes for dinner. They were good. As miserable as the whole werewolf situation was, at least he now had a metabolism to be envied. He decided to wash the sweets down with a beer, so he snagged a bottle from the fridge and spent a good fifteen minutes swearing steadily as he tried to find his bottle opener. When he finally tracked the damn thing down—tucked into his one and only oven mitt—he popped the top and wandered out onto the porch to drink and watch the rain.

When a figure came slogging through the puddles in his direction, Dylan felt an odd combination of hesitation and excitement. "Hey," Chris Nock said as he climbed the front stairs, a can of Budweiser in each hand. "I brought you a brew, but looks like you have your own." His T-shirt—a plain white one this time—was plastered to his body and nearly transparent, highlighting his broad chest and a pair of distractingly erect nipples. His hair was dripping onto his face.

"I was just finishing this one." Dylan set the empty bottle near the door—he had no intention to copy his neighbor's outdoor decorating scheme—and took the offered can. "Thanks."

"So it's okay if I actually show my face for a few minutes, huh? Long enough to play Welcome Wagon. I'm wearin' pants." He had this sarcastic little curve to his mouth that Dylan wanted to punch. Or perhaps kiss.

"I wasn't trying to be rude last time. I'm sorry."

"I get it. You like your privacy."

Dylan nodded and sipped at the Bud. He had to turn his head away when Chris tucked damp hair behind one ear. "Yeah," Dylan said. "It's pretty much why I moved out here."

"You mean you're not plannin' to run an organic winery or something? Grow heirloom tomatoes and quinoa? Grind your own wheat for bread?"

"I'm an architect." Dylan wasn't sure why he'd shared that information. It wasn't really any of this guy's business.

Chris chuckled. "Don't got a whole lotta those in the neighborhood."

They stood side by side for several minutes, staring out into the darkness. Chris wasn't quite close enough to touch, but Dylan could still feel him there, his proximity making the hairs on Dylan's arms stand up as if he were in an electric field. Dylan could smell him as well—beer and motor oil and cigarettes and a surprising floral scent that was probably shampoo or laundry detergent. The combination smelled rather nice.

Dylan's neglected cock twitched and considered coming to life.

"Fuck," Dylan mumbled.

"What? Tired of my company already?" Chris's smile hadn't faded.

"No. Sorry. It's been a long day, and I was thinking about how much I have to do before the place is really livable."

"Yeah, it's kind of a dump, ain't it?"

Dylan scowled at him, but Chris didn't seem to mean much with his snarky comments. He didn't seem to easily take offense either. He just kept on grinning and leaned his elbows on the railing. That particular position pushed his ass out in a way that was even more distracting than a wet T-shirt, and Dylan was thankful that the light was too dim for his flush or his half-hard dick to be noticeable.

"You got anyone yet to help you out?" Chris asked.

For a very brief moment Dylan thought Chris was talking about sex. Fortunately, his frontal lobe kicked in before his libido took over, and he realized the discussion was still centered on home improvement. He cleared his throat. "Not yet. I'm sure I can find someone."

"I used to work in construction, and my rates are reasonable. I won't even charge you for my commute time."

The offer took Dylan by surprise, and he had to process it for a minute. "But... won't you be busy... plowing?"

Chris stood straight and turned to look at him. Christ, that half smile was infuriating! "I didn't know you were interested in plowing," he said.

Dylan's face went redder. "I'm not. But it's spring and I figured you'd be planting stuff. Or something."

"Nah." He jerked his chin in the direction of his property. "I don't farm it myself. Lease it out to a guy who grows wheat. I just sit back and collect the bucks. Wouldn't mind a few extra dollars, though. I guarantee you—I'm a handy man."

Chris Nock was a gorgeous redneck who might or might not have been enjoying subtle double entendres at the faggot's expense. Dylan should have been kicking him off the porch and tossing his cans of crappy beer after him.

Instead, he heard himself saying, "Okay."

CHAPTER 4

DYLAN was still trying to decide where to plug in his coffeemaker when there was a pounding at the back door. He opened it, blinking bleary eyes at Chris Nock, who wore a pair of tight faded jeans and an equally tight and faded blue T-shirt. He had a leather tool belt around his waist.

"Mornin'," Chris drawled, grinning as if there was something amusing about Dylan.

"Um… morning. Come on in." Dylan stepped back and ran a hand through his uncombed hair.

Chris sauntered in and looked around the kitchen appraisingly. He smirked when he saw Kay's orchid on the counter, then turned to Dylan. "Where we gonna start?"

"Here, I guess. I wasn't expecting you quite so early. Hang on while I get the java going." Dylan took the coffeemaker into his future study and set it atop the mini-fridge. He had to come back into the kitchen to fill the carafe with water, and when he did he found Chris gazing thoughtfully out the windows at the soggy backyard. There was something lonely about the set of those broad shoulders, Dylan thought, and then silently chided himself. He was probably just projecting his own feelings onto his neighbor.

Dylan waited in the study while his coffee brewed, munching on a cupcake and no doubt scattering crumbs for the mice. Then he took his insulated mug and another cupcake back into the kitchen, where Chris was still at the window. "Want breakfast?" Dylan asked, holding the pastry out.

Chris looked down at the cupcake—white paper with red polka dots and pale blue frosting on top—and raised an eyebrow. "I ain't a ten-year-old girl, dude. I had sausage and eggs already."

Dylan scowled slightly. "Whatever. There's joe in the other room if you want it." Then he set his coffee down and ate the cupcake himself.

The other man didn't take him up on the half-hearted offer. Instead, he nodded his head at the toolbox Dylan had set in the corner. "You're payin' for my time. Wanna get going?"

"Yeah. Fine."

After a few minutes of discussion they decided that tearing out the cabinets would be a good place to begin. It was hard work, but it was also kind of fun to destroy things. Somewhere inside of Dylan, the wolf reveled in that bit of mayhem. Chris was a hard worker and clearly knew how to use his tools. It had been a very long time since Dylan had done physical work near another man, and he enjoyed it more than he remembered. He found himself frequently distracted, however, by Chris's rippling muscles or the little droplets of sweat that gathered on the man's face. Sometimes Chris would pause for a moment to swipe his hair away from his eyes with the back of one dirty hand, and Dylan would find himself wondering what it would feel like to run his fingers through that hair.

Neither of them spoke much as they worked, so the main sounds were hammers clanging on crowbars and the crack of wood breaking free. But sometimes Chris made little grunts of effort or chuckled when a piece of cabinetry proved especially stubborn, and Dylan would have to hide a smile.

They took a break midmorning. Dylan slumped on the floor against one wall, mug in hand, while Chris leaned against the remaining cabinet. "We need music," Chris announced.

"Sorry. My records and stuff are still packed away."

"Records? As in 'Golly gee, Gidget, come on over and listen to my keen new 45s'?"

"I like vinyl," Dylan replied loftily. "I mean, digital's okay, but it's a little… soulless. The little pops and scratches—those are more like real life. They have authenticity."

Chris rolled his eyes. "Whatever, dude. I bet a gramophone's even better. Or… what are those things? Those pianos that go by themselves?"

"Player pianos." Dylan chose to withhold the fact that a friend actually owned one.

Chris nodded and crossed the room, walking with his characteristic swagger. He kind of reminded Dylan of the roosters on the wallpaper, which Chris was currently picking at with his dirty fingernails. Then Chris turned around and cocked his head. "What d'you do when you ain't destroyin' your kitchen?"

"Told you. I'm an architect."

For some reason, Chris seemed to think that was funny. "You get paid to draw pretty pictures of houses."

"I get paid to *design* houses, yeah."

"That ain't so hard. You got walls, floors, a roof." Chris pointed around as he spoke. "Don't need no fancy college degree to figure that out."

"It's a little harder than making a box with windows."

Chris waved his hand dismissively. "Nah. Buildin' a house, that's the hard part. Puttin' the pieces together just right, draggin' beams around, workin' in the heat and rain."

Dylan stood up and crossed his arms over his chest. "I've done that part too. How do you think I knew how to tackle this job?" He had put in hours every summer during college, hanging up his barista apron to work construction because he thought the experience would help him understand architecture better.

"So you swung a hammer a few times. Big deal. There's guys, they do that every day for their whole lives, and they're just thankful for the paycheck, until one day they fuck up their backs too bad or screw up their knees, and they can't do it no more. And those guys never make anythin' near as much as the architects in their fancy suits and air conditioned offices."

"I don't wear a suit."

Chris nodded. "Yeah, I know. You buy your clothes at thrift stores because you want to prove that you're anti-corporate, and then you blow six hundred bucks on a porch chair made from repurposed wine barrels. I been off the farm once or twice, you know. I seen guys like you."

"You don't know me," Dylan spat back, irritated.

Chris worked his jaw but didn't say anything. He reached in his back pocket and pulled out a pack of Marlboros, but when he shook one out Dylan said, "Hey. No smoking inside."

Chris glared but stomped to the door. It slammed shut behind him, and Dylan peeked through the window. Chris was standing just outside in the drizzle, cigarette between his lips, hair hanging over his eyes. Dylan half expected him to go home. But instead Chris finished the cigarette and lit another, ground the butt under his boot heel when he was done, and flung open the door. Dylan pretended he'd been inspecting the window frame.

They got back to work, and at first the silence between them was oppressive. Dylan regretted the lack of music. But after a while they both loosened up a little, so that by lunchtime it was as if the argument had never happened. Dylan was relieved by the return to normalcy and also satisfied to see that Chris really did know his way around the job.

Chris went home for lunch, and Dylan ate a sandwich and the last of the cupcakes as he thought about his neighbor. He'd known from the start that Chris was eye candy, but to Dylan's surprise he kind of liked the guy. Yes, he was cocky and a little crude, but he was also refreshingly up-front, as if he didn't give a damn what people thought of him. Unlike other people Dylan knew, Chris certainly wasn't wasting any effort trying to impress with how much he knew or how he'd been into certain hip things long before they were cool.

Dylan wasn't sure why Chris was willing to spend time with him, other than the money. Actually, he'd never been sure why anyone wanted to spend time with him, unless they were family or they wanted a quick fuck.

Once upon a time, Dylan had dreamed of finding someone who could look past his skinny body, plain face, and general dorkiness and see the real him. Like a goddamn princess locked in a tower, he'd imagined his own Prince Charming coming to rescue him and to give him a happily ever after. It was a stupid thing to want—he'd known that even at the time—but he'd stubbornly held onto a little hope as he earned his good grades and got his good job and tried to live a successful life.

And then he'd met Andy, and those fairy tale dreams were destroyed. He'd gradually come to accept that he'd never get to settle for even the middle-class version of those dreams, the version with the honeymoon in Maui and the picket fence and the good-natured arguments over whose turn it was to mow the lawn. It broke Dylan's heart a little, but he'd succumbed to reality and acknowledged that those things would never be his.

He was a brave little toaster—now sharing his life with a wolf, he'd done what he could. He managed to keep his job, cage his new murderous impulses, and smile when Rick and Kay invited him over. He paid his taxes, hung out at bookstores, shopped at the Apple store, and read blogs. He'd made what he could of his life, and he'd told himself he was content, with only the niggling fear over others' safety keeping him from true happiness.

But that was a lie. Dylan was lonely. Not just for a lover—although he deeply yearned for one—but for a friend. Matty was cool and he had a nice time with her, but he could never quite let down his guard, never quite let her see what he was.

With all his hip urban friends and acquaintances, Dylan had never spent much time with anyone like Chris, but now he found himself wishing Chris could be his friend. "Idiot," he said to himself, just as Chris came walking back into his house.

"Just got here and already you're callin' me names," Chris said with a grin. He smelled of bacon and mayonnaise and chicken soup.

"Sorry. I was just… just remembering something I almost forgot."

Chris quirked an eyebrow at him and then shrugged. "Consider me clocked in."

They tore down the rest of the cabinets that afternoon, then removed the door between the kitchen and the dining room and dismantled the frame. Every now and then Chris would touch Dylan—a friendly pat on the shoulder here, an accidental brushing of hands there—and every contact made Dylan's stomach flutter. Dylan's muscles grew tired, but he wasn't about to admit it since Chris was still laboring away.

At a little past three o'clock, Chris went outside for another cigarette break. Dylan waited inside with his coffee, feeling both weary and wired. Little droplets of rain fell from Chris's hair when he came back inside.

Dylan walked over to the room's other doorway, which led to the hall. "I think I want to take down this door too. The opening isn't original to the house, and the door itself is a piece of crap." He rubbed at his little patch of beard thoughtfully. "Maybe I'll go with a curved arch instead of a square. You think you have the abilities for that?"

He turned to look at Chris and was surprised to be met with a glare. "Told ya I know what I'm doin'."

"Yeah, okay. It's just tricky, that's all. You can buy kits and stuff, and that's okay for the framing, but I think I'm going to look at an architectural salvage yard for the doors themselves. Find something more authentic, something decidedly unique."

"Of course you will," Chris said, confusing Dylan. What was his neighbor so pissed off about?

Dylan tried to smooth things over with a little babble. "I love old doors and how they have so much character. Or really, any interesting doors. My freshman year in college, I went on a trip to Barcelona—Spain—and we went on a tour of Casa Batlló. That's a house designed by this famous architect named Gaudí, who was sort of the father of Modernism and…." As Dylan spoke, Chris's brows had lowered and his expression had soured. Dylan let his little lecture peter out. "What?" he asked.

"You think I'm a moron, don't you?"

Dylan blinked at him. "Of course not."

But Chris's jaw muscles tightened. He looked away, then back again. "Sure you do. You think I'm an ignorant hick who ain't never heard of nothin' and who thinks that tractor pulls and monster trucks are high culture."

"I don't—"

"I *know* where Barcelona is, asshole."

"I'm sorry," Dylan said. "I just thought… I mean—"

"I know what you thought."

Dylan suddenly became angry. "You know what I'm thinking. You know exactly who I am. You must be a goddamn genius. Such a goddamn genius that you live in a shack in the middle of fucking nowhere and you don't have a real job and you can't even find your own goddamn toilet when you need to take a piss!"

They stood there staring at each other, both breathing hard, both with their hands balled into fists. For a few moments Dylan was sure Chris was going to come closer and take a swing at him. And then it hit him—the absurdity of it all: only one other human being as far as the eye could see, and Dylan had managed to alienate him within a single day. Dylan had to laugh.

"What's so fuckin' hilarious?" Chris growled.

"I am. We are." He filled his lungs deeply and let the air out, and was relieved to see Chris's tense posture soften. "Look, I'm sorry. I'm… my people skills aren't that great. I didn't mean to imply anything about your intelligence, okay? And I promise not to keep assuming that living in the sticks means you're inbred trailer trash if you'll stop supposing that I'm an asshole just because I grew up in a place big enough for traffic lights."

A hint of a smile played at the corner of Chris's mouth. "Can I still think you're an asshole for other reasons?"

"If I deserve it, you go right ahead."

Chris nodded slightly. He pulled the pack of Marlboros from his back pocket and seemed on the verge of shaking one out before he caught himself and put it away again. He shifted from one foot to the other. "I ain't sure this arrangement's gonna work out, dude."

Dylan felt an unreasonable sense of loss. "I said I was sorry," he said quietly.

"I know. Ain't all your fault." Chris gave him a long and appraising look. "I need to... think about this for a while. Figure some shit out." He barked out a laugh. "Maybe my people skills kinda suck too."

He strode across the room and opened the back door. But he paused in the doorway, one boot hanging in the air over the back step, and he turned to look back at Dylan. "See ya round the neighborhood, dude."

Dylan gave him a lame little wave. The door closed with a sound of finality, and the house seemed very quiet and achingly empty.

CHAPTER 5

IT WASN'T really a dream so much as a replayed memory, but it often came to him during sleep, right before the moon was full. It came to him tonight as he tossed and turned in his familiar bed in a still-unfamiliar room, his body sore from a day spent demolishing the old kitchen.

As always, it took place at Bleachers—a suburban sports bar that had seamlessly morphed into a meeting place for men, mostly in their thirties and forties, middle managers at Nike or workers at Tektronix or Intel. They wore Dockers and polo shirts and would have looked perfectly in place at a backyard barbecue. Nowadays the TVs flickered with images from MSNBC instead of ESPN, and the patrons would occasionally pair up and head back to the restroom together or leave the bar at the same time, but mostly the men sat and drank their Widmers and chatted quietly.

Dylan was a little younger than the average Bleachers customer, but he still went there every other Saturday or so. Ery Phillips—Dylan's friend from his Portland State days—used to call Bleachers *Geeks R Us*, usually right before he tried to drag Dylan to another downtown club with disco balls and naked boys on stages. Not that Dylan had anything against naked boys. It was just that, usually, well, he didn't have anything against naked boys. Ery's clubs were always full of guys who were cuter and better built and better dancers than Dylan.

The Bleachers guys were in his league, he figured. They didn't care that he bought his clothes at Urban Outfitters and would rather listen to Nirvana than Lady Gaga, that he was skinny and awkward and didn't own a single bottle of hair product aside from his shampoo.

Every once in a while Dylan would go with Matty and sometimes a couple of other people to Doug Fir, and the music there was usually pretty good. But Bleachers was where he went by himself, and, like him, it was boring but comfortable.

And then one Saturday night Andy came swaggering in—Dylan didn't know the guy's name yet, of course. Every head in the bar swiveled to follow the young god in the black leather jacket as he strode across the room. And no one was more surprised than Dylan when the new guy sat gracefully in the chair across from his.

"Hi. I'm Andy." The handsome man settled his big hands on the table.

Dylan tried to tear his eyes away from Andy's square jaw and deep brown eyes, from his flawlessly tanned skin, sensuous lips, and perfectly defined thick eyebrows. "Dylan," he replied, already kicking himself for sounding like an idiot.

But Andy leaned back in his chair and gifted Dylan with a slow smile. "It's nice to meet you, Dylan," he said, and when he flashed his very white teeth, Dylan felt a thrill course down his spine straight to his balls.

They exchanged a few words as Dylan finished his beer and Andy drank one himself, but Dylan could never remember afterward what they'd talked about. It didn't much matter anyway—Dylan was already giddy with lust, high on the knowledge that this stunning creature had chosen him. He stuttered a few sentences and tried desperately to look cool, but all the time he was marveling silently at Andy's incredible animal magnetism.

Hah.

Every eye in Bleachers was on them as Andy and Dylan left the bar and walked out into the clear August night, where the moon was waxing and a red and cream Indian was parked next to Dylan's suddenly pathetic Prius. Dylan wasn't the least surprised when Andy straddled the bike and revved the engine to life. "I'll follow you home," Andy had shouted over the roar.

DYLAN woke up in the farmhouse bedroom, sweaty and sore and hard as a rock. He jerked off quickly, fisting his cock furiously, hard enough to hurt, trying very hard not to think about Andy or anything related to him. What he ended up picturing instead was a twisted half smile, long hair hanging over blue eyes, a throaty sort of drawl, the scents of tobacco and cheap beer. He came with a strangled shout and then lay panting on his rumpled sheets. He wished he could simply stop his brain for a while, like shutting down a computer.

But Dylan's head was not a computer, and it wouldn't shut up. Eventually he stood and peered out his uncurtained windows. The sky was just lightening. He shambled off to his bathroom.

Over the past two days he had begun to wish he'd started with the master bath instead of the kitchen. Yes, he had a working toilet and sink and tub, but he didn't have a shower, which meant this morning he washed his hair under the tap and used a wet towel to wipe his body down. The hot water took a million years to make its way from the basement to the second floor, the mirror was cracked, and the entire room smelled slightly mildewed. Even though Dylan didn't have many toiletries, there was hardly room to store the few items he needed in the bathroom. His razor, deodorant, brush, and other bits were in a tangled, precarious pile on the single tiny shelf. Okay, for sure the bathroom was next. Including a rainforest showerhead.

Once he was dressed, Dylan made his way down the hallway, resisting the impulse to enter the yellow room and look out the window through the poplars. Downstairs, he began to brew some coffee. His kitchen might currently be rubble, but he needed his caffeine. He sniffed appreciatively as the wonderful smell began to fill the room. Coffee had always been one of his favorite scents, and his wolf's ramped-up olfactory abilities captured interesting nuances in the aroma.

With the first cup thrumming in his veins, Dylan began to haul debris out the back door and onto the soggy flat area that passed for a backyard. He would eventually have to rent a Dumpster, but that could wait. He was grunting and puffing, dragging the remains of an old cabinet down the three back steps, when he sensed someone watching him. He looked up with a smile—he'd been hoping against hope that Chris would turn up again—but his eyes widened when he saw who was coming around the house.

"Andy."

Andy stopped a few feet away. He was wearing his old leather jacket and a pair of tight black jeans, and his brown curls were plastered to his head from the helmet and the damp. "Looks like you got yourself a project."

"What the fuck are you doing here?"

Andy shrugged nonchalantly. "It's been a while. And there's a full moon tonight."

Dylan's arms were at his sides, his hands tightened into fists. "I told you I didn't want to see you again."

"No, you said not to come to your house again. And I didn't, right?" A bright flash of teeth. "You never said not to come here."

"Get out."

Andy raised his eyebrows and strode past Dylan, looking down the path that led to the pond. "Pretty sweet setup you got here. Lots of space to run." He took a few steps down the path and turned to look back toward the house. "And a big old house. Still telling yourself you're civilized, Dyl?"

Dylan considered going back inside and locking the door, but he wasn't at all sure that Andy wouldn't just skulk around the place and wait for him to come out again. Or maybe he'd just bust his way in. Dylan hated the way desire still coiled in his belly at the sight of his old lover, the way a part of him wanted to rip off Andy's tight clothes and rut against him in the rain. And he hated the way Andy smirked triumphantly, as if he knew exactly what Dylan wanted.

Andy's long legs quickly closed the space between them. "C'mon," he purred. He nodded his head toward the house. "Let's go inside. You can give me the tour. And then we can fuck. Just like old times."

Dylan's cock rapidly became so hard that the pressure in his jeans was uncomfortable. It was as if Andy's gravelly voice was a bell and Dylan was one of Pavlov's dogs, and wasn't that a fucking joke. "No," he said, but it lacked conviction.

"Yes," Andy said, leaning in close, his breath in Dylan's ear. He reached between them and pressed his palm against Dylan's groin, making him groan despite himself. "See? Definitely yes," Andy rasped. His hand still kneading gently, he dragged his tongue slowly beneath Dylan's jaw line.

Dylan shuddered. God, it had been so long. He remembered the heat of tanned skin atop him, the amazing ways that Andy could bend and move, the easy strength that kept Andy balanced over him on one arm while his free hand gripped Dylan's hair and his hips dove and twisted. His wolf remembered the feel of running alongside him with the wind in their faces carrying a thousand intoxicating scents, foremost among them the sweet smell of their prey's fear, and his muscles had bunched and—

"Fuck you!" Dylan shoved hard at Andy's chest, and the bigger man went stumbling backward. His feet slipped on the wet grass and tangled in some of the kitchen debris, and he fell back, hitting his head against a broken cabinet with a solid *thunk.*

As Andy scrambled awkwardly to his feet, Dylan bent and picked up a length of two-by-four. He didn't hold it threateningly, but his grip was hard, and his meaning was clear.

"You got a problem here?"

Dylan's head snapped to the side, and Andy almost lost his footing again as he spun in surprise. Chris was standing a few feet away, wearing honest-to-god overalls with his tool belt low on his hips like a gunslinger. He had a wide stance and a confident gaze, and it occurred to Dylan that this was a guy who'd probably been in a few fights. Unlike Dylan, whose last scrap was a playground brawl in third grade that ended with scraped knees and a trip to the principal's office.

For a moment, nobody moved. Then Dylan took a deep breath. "Hi, Chris. Andy's just leaving."

Chris nodded pleasantly enough, and Andy responded with a low growl, but then his shoulders slumped. He might just as well have rolled over and bared his belly, Dylan thought.

"Dylan, I didn't come here to fight," Andy began. "I don't know who this guy is—"

"Chris Nock. Neighborhood watch," Chris said with a grin.

"—but we need to talk."

Dylan shook his head. "No, we really don't. I'm done with you."

Andy actually winced, and Dylan almost felt sorry for him. Almost. Blood was running down Andy's neck and pooling around his collar. His clothes were smeared with mud. "Dylan," he began.

"Just go home, Andy. Go home, and don't come back. Ever."

For long, tense seconds Dylan wasn't sure how Andy would react. But finally his former lover hung his head and walked back around the side of the house, giving Chris a very wide berth and a hard glare. Dylan and Chris just stood there until they heard a motorcycle gun to life and speed away. Then they looked at one another. Dylan braced himself for harsh words, but all Chris said was, "Need some help in the kitchen today?"

They didn't get to work right away. First Dylan found a couple of towels so they could dry off, and watching Chris move the fabric over his body was pretty damn distracting. Evidently the little melodrama in the backyard hadn't cooled his libido much. There was more coffee—Chris liked his with milk, which Dylan didn't have, so he shrugged and took it black—and some discussion about the day's plans, and finally Chris helped demolish the rest of the wall and dump the pieces outside. They didn't discuss the morning's altercation or their disagreements from two days earlier, but Chris had a relaxed demeanor and a ready smile, and Dylan had the strange idea that his neighbor had reached some sort of decision.

By lunchtime they were both covered liberally in plaster dust, and they'd exchanged only a few dozen words. "Want a sandwich?" Dylan asked.

"Sure. Thanks."

Dylan washed his hands in the half bath, and then they both moved into the office-to-be for easy access to the little fridge. Chris watched silently while Dylan slapped aioli on stone-ground bread, added a pile of sliced prosciutto, and topped it off with Havarti. He handed one of the sandwiches to Chris. He noticed that, while Chris had scrubbed his hands pretty well, grease stains remained in the creases, and his fingernails were black.

"Getting your new cabinets and flooring and shit delivered's gonna be a bitch," Chris said with his mouth full. "Nobody likes to deliver out here, and they don't like taking their trucks down our road."

That thought had already occurred to Dylan. "Yeah. I guess I'm gonna have to rent a truck or something."

"Don't think you can cram a kitchen in your little toy car?"

"I can hardly cram myself in there. I think I need to buy a pickup."

Chris nodded. "Yep. Get an F-250, not one of them sissy trucks."

Dylan raised an eyebrow. "Sissy trucks?"

"Yep. Shiny things for weekend warriors to drive to REI. What you need is somethin' that can take a real load and haul a heavy trailer. And get one used, 'cause you're gonna end up with scratches and dents on it anyway."

"Thanks for the advice."

"Anytime. I won't even charge you for it." Chris swallowed the last of his sandwich and chased it with a slug of cold coffee. "But for bigger stuff, I got a flatbed we could use. It's not runnin', but I could get 'er goin' if you want."

"So you're a mechanic too?"

Chris gave his half smile. "I'm a man of many talents, dude."

Dylan decided he'd only imagined a flash of heat in Chris's eyes. Sunset was drawing closer, and all of Dylan's senses were beginning to go into overdrive, making him restless and slightly dizzy. And horny. Oh God, he was horny.

Without saying more, Dylan returned to the kitchen. With the wall to the dining room gone and all the cheap cabinetry taken away, the room was looking better than ever. But there was still plenty of work to be done before he could begin reassembly. The green vinyl floor needed to be pulled up, as did the brownish shag carpeting in the former dining room. Then they'd tackle that rooster wallpaper. *One thing at a time*, he reminded himself. At least with Chris's help the work was going a lot faster than he'd anticipated.

It didn't take them long to rip up the carpet, revealing scratched oak flooring beneath. "You gonna refinish this?" Chris asked.

"No, not in here. I want the whole room consistent. Usually I like bamboo or cork, but not for a house this old. I was thinking either maple or salvaged oak, but now I'm leaning to tile." He rubbed the back of his neck. "I guess I need to make up my mind pretty soon."

"Anything's gonna be an improvement, dude."

They moved to the kitchen area and started to peel up the vinyl, a much harder job than the carpet. Somebody had used some really good glue when they installed the ugly stuff. As Dylan sweated and winced at his raw fingertips, Chris was right beside him, sometimes humming tunelessly under his breath. Dylan had to be careful not to look at him too often or too long, because the sight of Chris down on his knees, hair hanging in his eyes, ass covered in worn denim and waggling temptingly, was almost more than Dylan could bear.

"Who was that guy?"

Chris had been silent for so long that Dylan startled a little at the question, and then it took him some time to formulate an answer. "An old mistake."

"You move out here to get away from him?"

Dylan snorted softly. "If so, I wasn't very successful, was I? Nah, he's not the reason I'm here. At least, not directly."

Out of the corner of his eye he could see that Chris was looking at him curiously, but Dylan was in no mood to elaborate so he changed the subject. "So, you grew up here?"

44

Chris paused a long time before answering. "I stayed here pretty often, with my gramps." There was something odd about his tone, as if the topic were uncomfortable. And then he yanked, pulling free a big section of flooring with a rip and a grunt. "Since we're sharing, what happened to your parents?"

"Car wreck. Big rig rolled over on the Terwilliger Curves and flattened their car. Dad was DOA, and Mom died a few days later." He'd recited this little tale dozens of times, but the pain still felt new and raw. Sometimes, though, he was almost glad the accident had happened. At least they'd been spared the heartache of their younger son getting himself turned into a goddamn werewolf.

"How old were you?" Chris asked.

"Eighteen. Freshman in college, so it wasn't like I got shipped off to an orphanage or anything."

"It's still a bitch."

"Yeah." Dylan dared another peek at Chris, who wasn't looking at him. "You?"

"Mom died when I was fifteen. Cancer."

"And your dad?"

"For all I know the bastard's still kickin'. Haven't heard from him since I was five or six."

"Oh." Dylan wasn't sure which was worse—a deadbeat father or one who was just plain dead. Either one sucked.

They labored for another hour after that without speaking more than a few necessary words. Dylan didn't often get to do physical work, and he rarely had a partner, so he was slightly startled to realize how much he was enjoying himself. Taking an armful of flooring out to the backyard, he was dismayed to see how late it had become. He trotted back inside, trying not to seem too panicked.

"Hey, I think I'm ready to call it a day," he announced.

Chris twisted around to look at him. "You sure? Another forty, fifty minutes and we'll be done."

"No, I gotta... I've got stuff to do. We'll finish it off day after tomorrow, okay? Tomorrow I'm busy." Well, more like recovering, but Dylan wasn't going to tell him that.

"You're the boss," Chris said with a shrug. He stood and stretched and twisted his back a little. Then he picked up his tool belt—removed because it was in the way when they were down on the floor—and buckled it around his hips. Dylan hovered near the back door. He felt like an asshole, just kicking the guy out like that, but he didn't have time for social niceties.

Chris sauntered by, and Dylan thought he was just going to leave without another word, but then Chris stopped and backtracked a few steps. "You don't have a TV," he said.

"Um… no." Dylan actually owned a television, but it was tucked in a box, and he hadn't bothered to unpack it yet. He didn't watch it that often.

"I do. Satellite."

Dylan stood there awkwardly, not sure how to respond. Chris rolled his eyes. "Do you want to come over tonight and watch it with me? After you finish your stuff. I got beer."

"I'm… uh… I can't. But thanks."

Was that really disappointment he saw flash across Chris's face? If so, it was gone very quickly. "Whatever, dude." Chris took a step toward the door.

"Wait."

Chris stopped and cocked his head a little. "Yeah?"

"Look, I probably should have…." Dylan paused and huffed impatiently at himself. "You do realize that I'm gay, right?"

The other man's mouth curled in amusement, and he crossed his arms on his chest. "Yeah, I kinda guessed that. Even before this morning's lovers' tiff."

"He's not my— It doesn't bug you?"

"Yeah, Backwoods Chris should be gatherin' his redneck buddies so they can kick yer faggot ass, huh? Or at least runnin' screamin' back to his shack before he catches your queer cooties."

Put like that it did sound pretty stupid, and Dylan was ashamed to have misjudged the man. "I didn't mean—"

But he was cut off abruptly as Chris moved forward, pressing his chest against Dylan's, forcing Dylan back until he was pinned against the peeling wallpaper. And before Dylan could gather his wits enough to push back, Chris was grabbing Dylan's hair in both fists, pulling his head down a little, and capturing his lips in a kiss forceful enough to hurt.

But it only hurt for a moment, a nice counterpart to the sweet twinge of tugging at his scalp. And then Chris's lips were soft and warm, his tongue was agile as it danced with Dylan's, and he tasted of rich, bitter coffee.

Dylan's dick had been restless all day, but now it surged to attention. Dylan found himself grinding his hips against Chris's, where a heavy thickness met his own.

When Chris pulled away, the smirk was back on his face, and Dylan was slightly breathless. "It don't bug me," Chris said.

Dylan gaped stupidly.

Like a cowboy who'd just captured the cattle rustlers, rescued the stagecoach, and foiled the bank robbery, Chris swaggered to the door.

"Chris!"

What Dylan wanted to say was *Stay. Stay here, in my home.* Or at least *Stay inside your own house tonight.* But he couldn't say either of those things, and Chris was waiting, eyebrows raised.

"See you on Wednesday," Dylan said.

That curl of the lips was already so familiar. "G'night, Dylan."

CHAPTER 6

USUALLY, fifteen minutes before the sun set on the night of the full moon, Dylan would be an anxious, pacing wreck. He would be locked in his safe room—his clothing already removed and carefully folded, waiting for him in his tidy bedroom—and he would be torn between the fear of escaping and the terrible urge to unlock the door.

Tonight he was naked and pacing, but that was where the similarity ended. Tonight he had the day's confusing events running through his brain in a muddled sort of way: the unexpected arrival of Andy and the altercation that had followed, the heady intimacy he'd felt working beside Chris, the kiss that had hit him more powerfully than a closed-fisted punch. And tonight the door was open—all the doors were open—so he could look outside and see the mist making the air thick, softening the line between day and night.

For the first time in over two years, and for only the second time since he'd been bitten, the wolf was going to run free.

It began with a maddening itch that made his skin twitch, that he knew he'd never be able to scratch. He shrugged his shoulders and tossed his head like a horse being pestered by flies. Then the ache began deep in his bones, first a dull thud in rhythm with his heartbeat and then a twisting, searing agony that made him grind his teeth to muffle his cries. But his teeth hurt too, and his entire jaw, and at the same time as his cock grew hard with excitement he fell to the floor and quivered there. His vision was hazy, reds and greens washing away and blues and yellows becoming paler. He heard sounds that had been hidden to him before—the squeak of rodents somewhere in the walls—

and as the sentient portion of his brain dimmed, he made a note that he'd need to buy traps.

It was always the smells that hit him like a bomb blast. When he thought about this later, it always reminded him of that moment when Dorothy lands in Oz, and her bland, sepia-toned world suddenly bursts into lush Technicolor. But maybe a Dorothy analogy was a little too clichéd for a gay man, and in any case, it didn't matter at the moment, when his entire sensory orientation had shifted wildly, along with the shape of his body.

More pain, so hot and sharp that he couldn't take it, he couldn't… but he did. One last shudder and an agile leap to his paws. The door was open, and the velvety darkness was calling to him.

Dylan ran.

Terrain that was steep and a little difficult on two feet was easy on four, and thick fur made an effective barrier against blackberry thorns. So many intriguing smells. And he wanted. He wanted, but he no longer had the words to shape his desire. He ran without planning or thought, just the joy of smooth muscles rhythmically stretching and flexing.

Down at the pond, small things splashed and slithered. Water was good—it would be cool on his warm, panting tongue, full of slippery life that would slide pleasingly down his gullet. But not yet. Now he squeezed through the underbrush and around the pond, then climbed the thick woods on the other side. He hadn't been this way before; there were no paths for human feet.

He bounded through the forest, leaping over fallen logs, stopping now and then to snuffle at the base of a tree or beneath some ferns. Twice he paused long enough to sit on his haunches and howl his freedom. A coyote answered back once, far away and defiantly fearful. Dylan ignored it.

But he didn't ignore the scent he caught—fast and warm and scared—and he put his nose to the ground and ran until he saw the rabbit. It was cowering under a sapling. Very still but not invisible. Dylan jumped.

Hot blood in his mouth, muscles and tendons and bones giving under his jaws. Wonderful.

Dylan had eaten a pound of raw hamburger before he changed, and although the cold meat alone hadn't been enough to satisfy his hunger, now his belly was full. He licked the blood from his muzzle and then spent several hours simply exploring, getting a feel for his new territory. Sometimes he lifted a leg and pissed on a tree. *Mine. I was here.*

He was a little footsore but happy when he returned to his pond. He took a long drink of the cold, green-tasting water. Then he padded quickly around the perimeter of his yard, pausing every several feet to mark his territory. He was going to go inside where it was warm and dry. But instead he darted through the poplar trees. He glanced with slight interest at the little house, at the collection of cars and trucks that huddled behind the house and smelled of old metal, at the splintery porch and piles of empty bottles and cans. The lights were on inside, and he could make out voices, then tinny laughter, followed by bright, bouncy music.

Dylan pissed on the corners of the porch and then, for good measure, around the edges of the weedy yard.

The back door to his own house was still open. When he got into the kitchen he shook droplets of condensation off his fur. In the hallway he found a bit of ham that he or Chris had dropped at lunchtime, and he snatched it up. He clambered up the stairs—not liking the way his nails slid on the slippery wood—and into his bedroom. He hopped onto his neatly made bed, turned around a few times, and, dimly thankful that for some reason the change back to human was considerably less traumatic than the change to wolf, collapsed into a deep and contented sleep.

CHAPTER 7

WHEN Dylan woke nude on his bed, there were grass stains and dirt on the duvet and grayish hairs clinging to his pillow. He had no idea how to enforce a no-animals-on-the-bed rule when he was both master and... pet. Or something.

But aside from the housekeeping issue, he felt better than he had in a very long time. That terrible yearning he usually felt the morning after a change was gone—the wolf had run and fed and was content to rest for a month. His memories of the previous night were jumbled, perhaps because wolf thoughts didn't set well in a human-shaped brain, but he knew he'd felt good and that the only casualty had been Thumper.

He also remembered nosing around next door, and his feelings about that were a little more unsettled. What had he been looking for? God, what if Chris had come outside, maybe to take a leak off his porch again, as he had every right to do. But he hadn't, and hopefully wouldn't that one night a month when the moon was full.

Dylan stood and stretched hugely. He was filthy and covered in countless fine scratches, especially over his belly where the fur had been a little thinner and the brambles caught him. He padded into the bathroom. While he waited for the water to heat and the tub to fill, he used the toilet, then brushed his teeth—ugh, fur in his molars—and looked down at his dick, which felt as languid as the rest of him.

His tub was huge, and the water felt wonderful. He couldn't remember the last time he'd had an honest-to-god bath. He wondered if purchasing scented salts would be too gay even for him. His mind meandered lazily to the house he was designing for the firm and to his intentions for his own kitchen. Of course that reminded him of Chris. He was sorry they wouldn't be working together today, although he didn't know quite what to expect the next time they faced each other. Had Chris been teasing him with that kiss? It sure as hell had felt authentic. Dylan had never known his gaydar to be so off, but then he'd never met someone like Chris before.

Since his turning a couple of years before, things had been difficult. First, it had taken Dylan several months to accept that he was now a werewolf. Yeah, he'd known that Bad Things Happened. If the fairly unpleasant process of coming out to his family hadn't taught him that, the sudden and premature deaths of his parents would have certainly driven the point home. Part of accepting what he had become had involved acknowledging the fact that he would never be able to have a serious love relationship. Which was ironic, considering that before the bite nobody had paid him much attention, and after the bite men seemed to find him irresistible. But even if he could ensure that his partner would be safe with him, how would he break the news of what he was? And what kind of crazy person wanted a werewolf as a boyfriend?

So Dylan had taken the safe route since the bite, ignoring his libido until he couldn't stand it any longer and then giving in to quick backroom fucks with men he'd never see again, men whose names he never bothered to learn. He was almost resigned to it, although nowhere close to happy about it.

But, Chris.

Well, even if he was serious about that kiss, he probably wasn't ready to pick out a wedding cake. Maybe he wanted a fuck buddy. Maybe Dylan would have to settle for that.

His happy mood fully soured, Dylan drained the water from the tub and went to get dressed.

HE SPENT most of the day scraping dried glue from the kitchen floor. It was arduous, frustrating work, and it made his back and knees and hands hurt. The little wounds scattered across his skin caught on his clothing as he moved. The reek of the ancient glue irritated his sensitive nose. He was tired and lonely and cranky and didn't even have anyone to whine to.

"Fuck this," he said somewhere around midday. He tossed the paint scraper aside with a clatter.

He stood and peered out the kitchen windows into the rain, then walked into the living room and stared across the road at the empty fields belonging to Chris. He supposed that by late summer they would be covered in golden blankets of grain. Now they were just drab and bleak.

He wanted a latte and Tillamook cheeseburger from Burgerville, and he wanted to hang out at Powell's bookstore, maybe catch a movie at the Baghdad.

He wanted to get laid.

During the afternoon, Dylan worked on the almost-completed house plans. He had a meeting at the office on Thursday morning. His boss and the clients would be there, and he hoped everyone would be happy. He'd probably go out to lunch with Matty afterward, maybe see if Rick and Kay were free for dinner. Maybe he'd go to Lowe's and pick out some kitchen flooring. He smiled—maybe he'd even go shopping for a truck.

"YOU got a lot done yesterday. Could've called me over to help."

Dylan told himself he shouldn't feel repentant about choosing to work by himself for a few hours. "I was going to do some other things but kind of got sucked in."

Chris grinned at him, which made Dylan blush. He was beginning to suspect his neighbor possessed a twelve-year-old's sense of humor. He cleared his throat. "So I was thinking we'd finish up the floor today and then tackle the wallpaper."

"Sounds like a plan."

Dylan had had enough of the awkward silences between them. He set up his laptop in a corner and accessed iTunes. Some heated negotiations followed—Chris had a fondness for '80s southern rock that Dylan didn't share—but they eventually reached a compromise that involved alternating Molly Hatchet with the White Stripes. Chris sang along out of tune, which Dylan found oddly endearing. Neither of them mentioned their kiss, and Chris was so nonchalant that Dylan began to wonder if he'd imagined that moment—maybe lust and the full moon had addled his head a little.

When their stomachs started grumbling, Dylan realized he had nothing to eat except bread and a couple of apples. Between the tiny fridge and the lack of a local grocery store, keeping the larder stocked was a pain.

"Come on next door," Chris said. "I'll make us somethin'."

Dylan hesitated a moment. But he really was hungry, not to mention curious about the inside of Chris's house, so he nodded. "Yeah. Okay."

They took a shortcut through the poplars. Dylan flushed again when they climbed onto the same porch where he'd lifted his leg the night before, but Chris didn't seem to notice. They entered the little house through the back door.

The living room was tiny and crowded with worn but comfortable-looking furniture. It was neater than Dylan had expected. Apparently his neighbor confined his beer can structures to the outdoors. There was a huge plasma TV, but there was also a bookshelf stuffed with well-read paperbacks: spy novels and mysteries mostly, but also quite a few by authors like Jack London, Kurt Vonnegut, Mark Twain, and William Faulkner. Chris caught him staring at the books and grinned. "Bet you thought I was illiterate too."

Dylan couldn't help but smile back. "Maybe more of a comic book type."

"*Watchmen,*" Chris said, pointing. "And *Sandman.*"

Dylan trailed behind Chris into a kitchen that looked like it hadn't been changed in decades. Between the table and chairs, the fridge, and an old-fashioned rolltop desk, there was barely room to move. But it was clean and smelled of paprika and bay leaves.

"Have a seat," Chris said, gesturing in the general direction of the chairs. "I know you ain't a vegetarian, but you're not gonna insist on organic, free-range, fair trade slow food, are you?"

"Meat. I could really go for some meat."

Chris laughed. He yanked things out of cupboards and the fridge, banged a few pans, and within a short time handed over a plate heaped with food.

"Pasta?" Dylan asked.

"Noodles. Noodles and sausage and… and eat up while it's hot."

Dylan scooped a forkful into his mouth. "Oh my God." It wasn't just that he was hungry—this stuff was really, really good.

Chris looked pleased and sat down to eat some as well. "I been cookin' for myself since I was a little kid. I'm good at it."

"Your mom wasn't much of a chef?"

"My mom wasn't around all that much. Booze, drugs, men. I learned to look after myself." Chris's voice was very matter-of-fact, and he was looking down at his plate. Then he got up abruptly and went to the fridge, finding a pair of Budweisers. He tossed one to Dylan, who caught it neatly and popped it open. Chris sat back down.

"That's why you spent time here with your grandfather?"

"Yeah. Sometimes she'd dump me off. Child Protective Services brought me twice. I hitched a few times. Gramps didn't really know what to do with me, but at least he didn't—" He stopped, made a sour face, and ate some more noodles.

"That's when you saw the old man in my house."

Chris seemed relieved at the change of topic. He leaned back a little in his seat and took a sip of his beer. "Yeah. Gramps's brother."

"What was with the staring through the window? That's kind of creepy."

"Your fairy real estate agent didn't tell you the whole story?"

"No."

"Uncle Frank went off to Korea, and while he was there Gramps knocked up Frank's girlfriend. By the time he got back they were married. I guess Frank couldn't forgive him for that. They never spoke to each other again, but they still lived next to each other." He gave a proud smile. "We're kinda known for being stubborn, us Nocks."

"Congratulations."

Chris gave a courtly, seated sort of bow, then stood and refilled Dylan's plate. Dylan dug right in.

"I don't know what was goin' through the old man's head when he was spyin' like that. Maybe he just wanted to get a glimpse of Marylee—that was Gram—but he kept on looking even after she was dead. I was four. Maybe he was just glad to see Gramps as miserable as he was. You know, first Marylee buried, then his asshole son takes off, and his daughter-in-law's a druggie and a whore." He shrugged. "And Gramps gets stuck with me. He wasn't a happy man."

Dylan imagined a young version of Chris, left with a bitter old man in a shitty little house in the middle of nowhere. "Sorry," he said.

Chris's eyes flashed angrily. "Wasn't looking for sympathy, dude."

There was a pretty awkward silence after that. Dylan polished off his second plate of food, and Chris finished his first. Chris seemed to have gotten over his momentary irritation because he laughed and pointed at Dylan's dish. "You want thirds?"

"Um… no. Thanks. I'm good."

"You can really put it away. What kind of workout do you do? Running?"

Dylan paused but then shook his head. "No, I don't really… I just have a good metabolism, I guess."

"Huh." Chris put their dishes in the sink and leaned back against the counter, sipping his beer. He set down the empty can and chewed on his lip thoughtfully. That was the first sign of real uncertainty Dylan had seen in the cocky man, and for some reason it made his heart twinge a little. Then Chris must have reached a decision because he nodded and smiled. "You're gonna have dinner here from now on, dude. 'Til your kitchen's done."

"I couldn't—"

"Guy who eats like you shouldn't be tryin' to survive on cornflakes or whatever the hell you been eatin', and cookin' for two ain't no more work than for one."

Dylan hesitated and thought he saw a flash of pain in those fierce blue eyes. "Okay. I'll split your grocery costs," said Dylan.

"Done," Chris said with a wide grin.

"How do you have time for all this? The cooking, the—" Dylan waved his hands vaguely in the direction of his house. "—the construction, the mechanic stuff. Don't you have a regular job?"

"Sometimes." He rummaged in a cupboard for a moment, emerging with a pack of Marlboros and a blue plastic lighter. Dylan watched in fascination as he patted the bottom of the red and white box, pried the top open, pulled out a cigarette, and placed it between his full lips. His thumb flicked a flame into life, and he took a long drag, then exhaled a thick cloud of smoke. "I don't owe nothin' on the house or the land, and I get cash off the guy who rents the fields. When I start runnin' low, I find somethin' for a while. Like workin' for the sucker who bought the dump next door." He grinned and tapped his ashes into the sink.

"But what if you couldn't find a job?"

Chris shrugged. "Always have."

"But what if you got hurt or something? Do you have insurance? And how about retirement?" Just the idea of being without a financial safety net made Dylan feel mildly panicked, despite the good benefits through his job and the bulk of his parents' life insurance payout tucked away in Treasury bills and long-term CDs.

But Chris looked amused. "I ain't gonna worry 'bout none of that shit unless it happens."

"But you have to—"

"Dude. Chill. I just deal with things when they come." He looked so relaxed with his cigarette and his too-long bangs and the strap of his overalls falling off one broad shoulder.

Dylan gave an embarrassed little smile and stood, rubbing his stomach. "Maybe we should get back to work."

Chris took a few more drags of his cigarette and then stubbed it out in the chipped enamel of the sink. They both reached the doorway at the same time, and Dylan stepped back slightly to let him pass. But Chris turned very suddenly and grabbed Dylan's arms and *bang!* Dylan again found himself pressed to the wall by Chris's solid bulk. This time it was Dylan's hands that clutched at hair, fingers tangling in strands that were surprisingly soft, and he bent his face down for a long, heated kiss.

Chris made a sort of humming noise into Dylan's mouth and slid his hands over Dylan's biceps and then down his sides until they settled near Dylan's waistband. His broad fingertips kneaded at Dylan's flesh and tugged Dylan's hips forward so they could feel each other's heat and hardness, so they could rock and grind just a little for sweet friction.

Dylan shouldn't have been surprised at this turn of events. Hell, a part of him had been hoping for this since Chris had invited him over. Yet somehow he felt astonished to have this weight against him, to be tasting another man's hunger as bright and sharp as his own. His fingers tightened their grip, and Chris groaned and thrust hard.

Suddenly, Dylan wanted—no, *needed*—bare skin. He released Chris's hair and pushed the overall straps down. Chris pulled slightly away, breaking the kiss, but only so he could work at the buttons of Dylan's shirt. Arms tangled a bit in their sudden desperation, and one of Dylan's buttons popped off, but soon the overalls were in a puddle at Chris's feet, and Dylan's shirt was tossed to the side and each of them was trying to tug a T-shirt over the other's head.

As soon as their torsos were bare, they were back against one another, chest to chest and lips to lips. Chris pulled at Dylan again, making sure there was enough space between Dylan and the wall for Chris's hands to wander over his back and shoulders. His fingers were rough, the calluses dragging across skin in a way that made Dylan shiver. Dylan's hands were just as busy. He slid his palms along smooth muscle and caressed shoulders. He made Chris shiver in turn when he ran his fingers firmly along the bony ridge of spine.

Dylan buried his nose in Chris's hair, inhaling deeply. He wondered vaguely if he could become drunk off the rich odors of drugstore soap and hard work and spicy meals, and a scent that spoke eloquently to him of Chris's desire and need.

When his hands moved down, squeezing an ass that was spectacular even in plain white briefs, Chris groaned, moved his head a little, and nibbled lightly at Dylan's pebbled right nipple. Dylan gasped, and Chris raised his head, smirk in place but pupils wide. "C'mon," he said. His voice was hoarse. He bent and pulled his overalls high enough so they weren't hobbling him, and with his free hand he grabbed one of Dylan's.

Maybe Chris meant to take them to the bedroom, but they didn't make it that far. They ended up against the back of the couch, those damn overalls back down around Chris's ankles, Chris's fingers fumbling at Dylan's fly. Just that light pressure alone was almost enough to send Dylan over the edge. It had been a long while since anyone else had touched him.

"God… Chris… please…." he panted.

Chris chuckled throatily and pushed down Dylan's jeans and boxers. Dylan squeezed his hands under the back waist of Chris's briefs. They both moaned when he finally made contact with the ass he'd first admired from the window next door. Dylan squeezed hard, causing Chris to buck forward and press their cocks together, the already damp cotton of his underwear a maddening barrier.

"Fucking gorgeous," said Chris, flexing his butt in Dylan's hands. "So goddamn hot even with that stupid caterpillar on your chin."

Dylan was lightheaded with the surfeit of sensation, but Chris's gibe made him laugh, and he pulled one of his hands free to slap playfully at Chris's rump. Chris laughed in return, then wiggled, making them both serious again: kissing, humping, breathing hard. Sweat gathered along Chris's neck, and Dylan couldn't help but lick it off. "You taste good." Chris's reply was just a rumble against Dylan's chest.

The fabric between them became too much, and Chris's briefs were nearly torn as they both tugged them down. Chris's chest was almost hairless, and only a soft line led from his navel to his groin, but the curls at the base of his cock were lush and thick, darker than the hair on his head. He had no tan lines—and didn't seem the sort to hang out at SunsUp or Tan Republic—so his lovely light caramel coloring must have been natural. His cock was like the rest of him: not too long, but nice and thick. Dylan would have liked to admire it more closely, and he really wanted to bury his nose in those curls and between those solid thighs, but Chris was squeezing their dicks together, and it felt good.

Very good, actually, especially when he gave his wrist a little twist and rubbed his broad thumb over the wet heads. Dylan's hips bucked forward into the heat and pressure. "J-Jesus."

Chris braced himself back against the couch—Dylan's hands trapped comfortably between his butt and the nubbly fabric—and threw his head back, eyes closed. His neck was corded, bitable, his lower lip caught between his teeth. He balanced his left palm on the point of Dylan's hipbone but didn't grab, just letting his hand ride along as Dylan rocked forward and back.

Their breathing was very loud in the small room, Chris's pubic hairs tickled against the crease of Dylan's thigh, and the scents were so strong and musky and sweet that Dylan had to squeeze his eyes closed.

Heat was running along his back, pooling at the base of his spine, sending sparks into his belly and legs and balls. "Fuck," Chris moaned. "That's so good."

Dylan couldn't feel his feet and didn't care. He was trembling now, hips jerking fast, pounding hard enough against Chris to drive the couch forward several inches. "Like... yeah, like that," he said when Chris gripped their cocks just a little more tightly. Then he couldn't say anything at all, white flashing behind his closed lids, knees wobbling dangerously.

"Dylan!" More of a grunt than a yell.

Sticky slickness between them, a salty living scent filling Dylan's nose, like blood, so like blood.

Chris released them both and then, to Dylan's surprise, grabbed his shoulders and kissed him again, this time slow and soft. He pulled away, looked down at their torsos, and laughed. "I think we need a towel."

It took them a few minutes to clean up and dress. All the while, Chris hummed to himself. The rain had begun again, so they dashed between the poplars, laughing as mud squished and wet branches slapped at them.

Dylan was a little worried about the rest of the afternoon. With the notable exception of Andy, he had rarely spent time with a partner once the orgasm had faded. He didn't know if things would be awkward between them now, whether Chris might be feeling regret.

But his fears proved unfounded. The wallpaper came off in tiny, crumbly bits instead of large sheets, but the companionable cooperation built over the past few days of work remained. They joked and teased and squabbled over the soundtrack, and by the time they headed to Chris's house for dinner, the kitchen walls were bare. And Dylan was happier than he'd been in ages.

CHAPTER 8

"DO YOU cook like this all the time?" Dylan asked with his mouth full.

"Yeah. Well, every couple of days, and then I nuke the leftovers. I take it you don't, even when you have a stove?"

"No. I can do a few things—a guy's got to if he lives alone—but mostly I do frozen or takeout."

"So why are you buildin' yourself such a fancy kitchen?"

Dylan hadn't really thought of that. "It's not that fancy."

Chris waved his hands. "Fancier than mine."

"I guess. It's just… a nice house is supposed to have a nice kitchen."

"There's no supposed to, dude. It's your place. Stick a hot tub in the middle and hang Astroturf on the walls—nobody's gonna complain." He cocked his head a little. "Unless you're just fixin' up the place so you can sell it for a profit. Like that show on TV."

"You watch TLC?"

Chris looked slightly embarrassed and stabbed at his pork chop. "Not the point."

"Well, I'm not planning to flip the house. I told you—I want to live—" He almost said *by myself*, but that wasn't quite right under the circumstances. "I want to live in the country."

"You'll get tired of it. Once the house is all done you're gonna realize there ain't nothin' much to do out here, and the nearest Asian fusion restaurant or microbrewery is sixty miles away, and you're gonna leave." He was sawing angrily at his meat, not making eye contact.

"I won't get tired of it."

"But you won't explain why you want to be alone."

Dylan squirmed uncomfortably in his seat. "Nothing to explain. I like quiet."

"Huh." Chris wiped his mouth with a paper napkin, then wadded it into a ball. And then whatever anger he'd been feeling seemed to drain away, and he gave his half smile. "So your shiny new stove is gonna be kinda like those throw pillows with the little tassels. Nobody ever uses them for nothin'—they just cost a heap of cash and look pretty."

Dylan blushed a little and decided Chris didn't need to know he had actually kept a number of throw pillows on his bed until he moved. "Tell you what. You can come over and cook me dinner on my fancy new stove."

"Yeah?" Chris raised a single eyebrow. "You figure you're gonna get a chef and a handyman and a piece of ass out of the deal?"

"If I'm lucky. Oh, and a mechanic too. Don't forget that."

Chris snorted noisily and watched Dylan start his second serving of sautéed vegetables. When the meal was done, Dylan washed their plates and stacked them on the gold-flecked Formica countertop while Chris sat and smoked. Dylan turned to look at him. "I should go."

That little flicker of emotion crossed Chris's face—whether anger or fear or disappointment, Dylan wasn't sure. Chris didn't say anything, though. He just lit another cigarette.

"I have to wake up early tomorrow. I have a meeting in the city."

"I ain't stoppin' you."

Dylan waited a moment, then nodded. "Well, thanks for dinner."

His only answer was a cloud of smoke.

He went through the living room—carefully not looking at the couch—and out the back door. He still hadn't been through the front door, and he hadn't seen Chris's bedroom. He stepped out onto the back porch and stood there with the drizzle in his hair, dripping down his collar and into his eyes. And then he turned around and walked back into Chris's house.

Chris was sitting at the kitchen table with his shoulders slumped. He looked up sharply when Dylan entered the room. "Forget somethin'?"

"Yeah." It took only a few strides to cross the little room. Dylan set his hands on Chris's shoulders, leaned down, and snuffled his hair. "I really do have to turn in early tonight," he whispered. "But Friday we can get some more work done, and then I can stay up as late as I want."

"Maybe I have plans Friday."

Dylan didn't release him. "Saturday then."

"Maybe I want the weekend off."

"What if I pay you time and a half?"

Chris tipped his head up to look at him. He was smiling. "Asshole."

THE radio was tuned to NPR, but Dylan wasn't paying attention to *Morning Edition*. As he piloted the Prius down the seventy-mile route that was already becoming familiar, his mind was on the events of the day before.

He knew why he'd had sex with Chris—the guy was hot as hell, and Dylan was desperately horny. What he didn't understand were his feelings afterward: guilt for not sticking around after dinner and accepting Chris's unspoken invitation to fuck again, and worry that he'd hurt Chris's feelings. He knew he was stupid to feel that way. A little frotting did not equal a marriage proposal. And Chris was... opportunistic. He'd practically admitted that himself. Dylan was a chance for him to pay some bills and get off a few times, and that was all. Not that Dylan blamed him for that attitude.

Besides, Dylan knew full well that he was in no position to form any kind of attachment to another person.

He zoomed down the highway past trees with fresh new leaves, and he thought about how fucked his personal life had always been. He hadn't dated at all in high school. He had still been somewhat in denial about being gay—or maybe just afraid to climb out of the closet—so he'd kept his nose buried in books. His horizons had expanded a little his freshman year in college, but that had led to the mortifying moment when his mother walked in on him and his biology lab partner during one of their "study sessions." Not long after that had come the grief over his parents' deaths, the hectic schedule of school, and—he'd convinced himself—no time for anything more than quick, back-room blow jobs.

Traffic slowed to a crawl as he arrived at the suburbs. Sandwiched neatly between a Ford Excursion and a furniture delivery truck, he returned to his reverie, remembering those couple of years after architectural school, when he was building his career. Designing houses for other people. Still too busy for a commitment. Still too forgettable for any first date to turn into a second.

And then he was twenty-seven, an age when his straight friends were getting married and his gay friends were beginning to talk about civil unions and domestic partnerships—and Dylan had never yet had a real boyfriend.

Until Andy walked into Bleachers.

Dylan, lonely and feeling left behind in the game of life, had been starry-eyed over such a beautiful man choosing *him*. And the sex that night had been mind-blowing. So when the next morning dawned and Andy was still gorgeous and the sex was still red hot, Dylan hadn't uttered a word of complaint when the virtual stranger basically moved into his place. In fact, for the first time in his life he'd thrown caution to the winds, calling in sick for several days running and spending his days and nights fucking on every surface in his house.

Until the night of the full moon.

Not that Dylan realized the moon was full that night. He didn't pay attention to that little matter back then. But whether he knew it or not, the moon was indeed full, and Dylan awoke from a postcoital doze to the sounds of muffled screams. He had rushed into the living room—still naked—and what he saw froze him in his tracks.

His lover was turning into a wolf.

Which was impossible, of course. Dylan had pinched himself, suspecting it was a dream, or maybe a hallucination. Perhaps Andy had slipped some kind of drug into his mochaccino. But the creature was there, as big as life on his Ikea rug, twitching and growling and... changing. Dylan was still standing there and goggling when the wolf climbed to its feet and swung its head to stare at him.

Dylan gathered enough wits to run.

He was aiming for the back door but made it only as far as the kitchen when the beast caught up with him. It leapt, sinking its huge fangs into the meat of his left calf. Dylan shrieked and tumbled to the floor. He would have been done for except that, as he fell, he knocked his Le Creuset French oven off the counter. Dylan had rarely used the pot, but he liked the way it looked on the stovetop. The pot banged onto the bamboo flooring and bounced, startling the wolf enough for it to release its grip. Dylan grabbed the pot, used it to bang the wolf on the muzzle, and then fled. But the floor was slippery with his blood and he doubted he could make it to the exit, so he dove instead into the butler's pantry and slammed the door shut.

The pantry hadn't been original to the house. Dylan added it when he reconfigured the kitchen. And because he was an eco-friendly kind of guy, he'd repurposed the discarded entry door from a reno project at work. Fortunately, the door was steel, and it withstood the animal's repeated bashing.

Dylan spent the night cowering in his pantry, naked and bleeding.

The next morning, Andy was gone. Dylan went to the ER and made up a story about a dog attack while he was jogging. He sat through stitching and bandaging and multiple forms. Then he returned to his silent, empty house.

Such was the history of his one and only stab at a lasting relationship. Well, unless you counted what happened when Andy reappeared four weeks later. But Dylan really didn't want to think about that, and it was with considerable relief that he parked the Prius in the underground garage at work and shut off the engine.

DYLAN'S boss wore designer jeans and black turtlenecks, even when meeting with clients. He had thick gray hair and John Lennon glasses, and he liked to talk about Kierkegaard and Wittgenstein as if they were his boyhood pals. Everyone—even his wife—called him by his last name, Stender.

Stender was sitting in his Eames chair in front of the glass-topped desk that was empty except for his MacBook, and he was smiling. "You did a fine job with the Maywood Drive project, Dylan. The clients were very pleased."

"Thanks." Dylan had to fight not to grin like an idiot. Stender didn't hand out praise very often. But the morning had gone well. The clients loved his plans, and they were especially pleased at the way he'd designed the deck around some of the big trees on the property.

"To be honest, I wasn't too keen on the idea of you telecommuting. I know you've agreed to come in for meetings, and you've always been good about deadlines, but I thought it might be a bad thing for you to be working out of this environment. Away from the creative wellspring." Stender could talk about things like creative wellsprings and keep a straight face. "But it seems that the wilderness has inspired your muse, if your latest work is any indication."

"It's… quiet there. I can think without a lot of interruptions." Aside from sexy neighbors.

"Well, and I suppose the grandeur of nature herself suggests balance and flow and sustainability."

"Right," Dylan said, not pointing out that at the moment the grandeur of nature mostly suggested mud and moss.

"Good then." Stender slapped his palm on the glass. "I have a new project I've selected especially for you. It'll give us a chance to see just how well this arrangement is going to work."

Dylan's stomach twisted. Stender had initially been fairly agreeable to his new work schedule, and it hadn't occurred to Dylan that there would be some kind of test. What if he failed? Then he'd be forced to choose between giving up his farm or quitting his job. "I'll do my best," he said.

"I don't doubt it." Another slap on the desk. "Matty has the files, and she can fill you in on the details." He stood and offered his hand, which Dylan shook.

Dylan and Matty decided to have a late lunch. They took her car to a little sandwich place near the approach to the Fremont Bridge. The tables were made of knotty planks, and the seats were long benches. The walls were hung with old produce crate labels. You had to order and pay at the counter and then fetch your own food when they called your name. But the roast beef was piled densely atop homemade herb bread, and the corn chowder was thick and slightly spicy.

"This is great, Matt," he said, swallowing an enormous bite.

"I know. I bet you haven't been eating like this out in the sticks."

"Um... no."

But maybe he blushed a little, because Matty's eyes narrowed, and she tilted her head a little. "What's up, Dyl?"

"Nothing. I gutted the kitchen so, yeah, not much cooking."

"That didn't take you long."

"Not much to distract me out there."

"Hmm." She slurped at her Mr. Pibb. "So is that all you've been doing? You haven't met any handsome lumberjacks or anything?"

"No, Matt. Paul Bunyan hasn't knocked on my door yet."

She still looked slightly suspicious, so he decided to change the subject. "So what's with this new thing Stender has for us?"

"Stender has for *you*, you mean. You're supposed to be idea boy. I just go along with the flow, boss."

"And you're okay with that?"

"More than. Wait 'til you see this one."

There was that knot of worry again. He put down his sandwich. "Why?"

"The clients are a pair of old hippie types—lesbians—who apparently stopped toking up long enough to make a small fortune off magic futons or something."

"Oookay...."

"They're big into alternative everything and Gaia theory and universal energies and... I don't know. All that stuff. And they want to build a big honking house in Beaverton."

"Beaverton?" That was a suburb more suited to the minivan-driving, mall-shopping, gym-going set than hippie millionaires.

"Yep," Matty replied smugly. "Oh, and they have dogs. Don't forget to design for the dogs."

Dylan was tempted to bury his face in his arms. The firm did get occasional eccentric clients, but they weren't usually routed his way. He got the West Hills yuppies and the Lake Oswego mini-mansions. People who wanted good design and high quality, but nothing too radical or eccentric. His clients were the type who hyperventilated at the thought of violating zoning ordinances. Stender must have sent this one his way either in some misguided attempt at tapping into homosexual solidarity—the clients were, after all, lesbians—or because he wanted Dylan to fail.

Dylan must have groaned, because Matty patted his hand. "You'll do fine. We're supposed to meet with them in two weeks, and they want rough plans then."

He tried to smile at her, but really he was calculating how long he could live off his savings if he ended up unemployed and what the job market was like for washed-up architects in rural Oregon. Of course, he could always move back into town and reinforce a spare bedroom again. And hope he always made it home on time. And never again experience that wonderful feeling of freedom and power when the moon was full.

His appetite was gone. He watched as Matty finished her lunch, and then they walked back to her car. He stopped in at the office only long enough to pick up the files. He didn't even look at the contents, other than to glance inside to see what the site address was. As he shuffled back to the Prius, he decided to ignore the job entirely for now, aside from scoping out the location on his way home. As originally planned, he'd spend his afternoon with the considerably less intimidating prospect of choosing his kitchen furnishings.

Several hours later, his cabinets and countertops were on order, and his mood had improved. He'd also picked up enough paint for the kitchen—Fernwood green—along with the necessary painting supplies. He was looking forward to that particular task. He loved the smell of fresh paint and the way just a couple of gallons of the stuff could transform a room so completely.

He ended up driving around Beaverton for twenty minutes in the dusk as he searched for the job site. Finally he found it—a large, flat lot in a neighborhood where all the streets had cowboy names. The neighboring houses, all unremarkable ranches and split entries, had been built in the '70s and early '80s. He couldn't imagine why the clients had chosen this particular location. The empty space was a little like a blank sheet of paper, with the topography and surroundings giving few hints for his design. He could put anything there. The question was whether he could draw something to satisfy the clients and his boss.

He squeezed his eyes shut for a few seconds, let loose a deep sigh, and turned the Prius toward home.

CHAPTER 9

THE pounding at the back door startled Dylan enough that a little coffee splashed out of his mug. He swore under his breath and stomped across the floor, and was then relieved to find Chris on the doorstep, half grin in place. "Mornin', sunshine," Chris said. He was wearing faded jeans and a T-shirt advertising Coors, a thick plaid shirt apparently serving as his coat.

Dylan leaned in the doorframe. "I thought you were busy today."

"My secretary found an opening."

They both waited in a sort of stubborn détente until Dylan yielded, moving out of the way so Chris could enter. "Coffee?" he asked.

"Nah, I'm good." Chris looked around and spied the supplies Dylan had bought the previous afternoon. "Paintin' today?"

"That was the plan. Unless... do any of those piles of rust behind your house actually run?"

"Sometimes. Why? Plannin' to run away?"

"Just as far as the nearest home improvement store. We could buy tile today."

"Sure," Chris said with a grin. "Road trip."

Fifteen minutes later they were climbing into an ancient Chevy truck that roared and grumbled like an angry dinosaur. "Radio don't work," Chris announced as they bounced down the gravel road. "Heater don't work neither, but the engine'll warm us up pretty good."

Dylan was warm enough already with Chris only inches away on the bench seat. Inside the cab of the pickup all the smells Dylan had come to associate with Chris were very strong: soap, cigarettes, oil and gasoline, denim, sweat.

"Allergies?"

Dylan looked at Chris in confusion. "Huh?"

"You were sniffin'."

Turning his head to hide his blush, Dylan said, "Just an itch, I guess."

Although the sky was a leaden gray, it wasn't raining. Chris was humming again—something by Lynyrd Skynyrd—and Dylan realized that, apart from his little lunchtime jaunts with Matty, it had probably been years since he was a passenger in someone's car. It reminded him of when he was a little kid, squabbling in the back seat with Rick as the family drove to the coast for the weekend.

"How about if I buy you lunch?" he said out of the blue. "Before we buy the stuff."

"Sounds good."

They didn't speak again for a long time, but Dylan slowly crept his hand across the seat until his pinky was almost but not quite rubbing against Chris's pants, and he watched the way Chris's hands moved on the steering wheel and the way his blue eyes scanned the road before them. Eventually the fields and woods gave way to subdivisions and strip malls, and when they turned off the highway Dylan directed Chris through city streets.

"What's this place?" Chris asked suspiciously when they climbed out of the car.

"Brewpub. It's good."

"I figured we'd just end up at Burger King or somethin'."

"Hey, you're the chef. You know we can do a lot better than that."

Dylan had been here before and knew it was slightly upscale, as brewpubs went, but that their casual clothes wouldn't be too out of place. The hostess smiled pleasantly at them, but when their waiter arrived he practically plopped himself in Dylan's lap. Chris scowled as they ordered fish and chips and pints of ale.

"You get that all the time?" he asked after the waiter reluctantly left them.

Dylan sighed. "Sometimes."

Chris's frown deepened, and they didn't talk as they waited for their food to arrive. Once they began to eat, though, Chris seemed to defrost a little. "You're right. This is better than BK. I guess you used to eat in places like this all the time."

"Pretty often, I guess. You don't go out much?"

"Not a whole lotta choices near home, dude."

"No. But, I mean, you do go out sometimes, right? For a burger or a beer?"

"I ain't a hermit." Chris chuckled. "I get out into the world now and then, have me a look-see at all them newfangled inventions like cellular phones and personal computin' machines." He stole two of Dylan's french fries and crammed them in his mouth. *Why are my fries always fair game?* Dylan wondered.

"I don't think you're a hayseed, Chris. Not anymore. I was just wondering what you do when you're not... swinging a hammer."

Chris looked down at his fingers, which were rolling the edge of a napkin. "I do things. Go out. Sometimes I just get in my truck and drive. No plan or anythin'. Just see where the road takes me, you know." He looked up at Dylan. "You ever do that?" Dylan shook his head.

They finished their food, and the waiter came by with the bill. Dylan ignored the googly eyes again. He paid but didn't get up right away, and neither did Chris. Finally, Dylan ventured a question he'd been wondering about for some time. "What do you do when you want to hook up with someone? Aside from offering to help him remodel, I mean."

"There's places," Chris answered vaguely. "You didn't move in next to the only faggot in Columbia County. That rest stop over on

Highway 47, sometimes you can get lucky out there. I wasn't a blushing virgin when we met, dude."

Dylan grinned at him. "You seemed to know what you were doing."

That made Chris leer so heatedly that Dylan's cock stirred. "Let's go," he said, standing abruptly. Chris laughed and waggled his fingertips at the waiter as they walked to the door.

Home Depot was fun. Dylan picked out a couple hundred square feet of ceramic tile for the floor and a coordinating pattern for the backsplash. Then he got bags of mud and grout, spacers, plastic barrels, a mixer blade for his drill, and a couple of trowels. The big splurge was a midrange tile saw. He winced a little when it was time to pay the bill, but Chris was almost bouncy. "I like your tools," he said, helping to load the truck with their purchases and stopping to slap Dylan's ass.

Traffic was slow as they headed home, but Dylan didn't mind. He liked sitting next to Chris, listening to him sing, feeling the engine rumble. They chatted on and off, mostly about their construction plans for the next day. But as darkness fell they grew silent, and the cab became somehow more intimate, the air thicker, the heat enough to fog up the windows and create little beads of sweat on their scalps that dripped down their necks. By the time Chris pulled the truck around to the back of Dylan's house and cut the engine, they might have been the only two people left on earth.

They sat in the dark of the cab, just breathing.

Then Chris twisted a little in his seat and set a heavy hand high on Dylan's thigh. "God, I want you," he whispered.

Dylan was slightly embarrassed as a needy little whimper escaped his throat, and then they were kissing hard enough for teeth to clack, and Dylan's hands were fisted in Chris's hair, holding him tight. Most of Dylan's previous sexual experiences hadn't involved much kissing, and he'd never before realized how much it could feel like fucking when a tongue penetrated his mouth, how the taste of another man could make his balls tingle and his skin feel tight and hot.

When they pulled apart, panting, Chris's teeth gleamed in the darkness.

They fumbled at one another's clothing, and Chris half straddled him, but the front seat of a Chevy didn't offer much room for two grown men. The gear shift was jammed uncomfortably into Dylan's leg, while half his body was pinned under the big steering wheel. "Let's take this inside," he suggested.

Chris kissed him again—this time fast and teasing—and opened the passenger side door. They both tumbled out, nearly ending up in the mud but just barely managing to keep their feet by grabbing at each other and the truck. Dylan's dick was so hard that it actually hurt to run, but neither man wasted any time rushing into his house. Chris looked around curiously when they got upstairs. It occurred to Dylan that Chris hadn't seen the second floor yet, although this was no time for a tour. He tugged at Chris's sleeve and dragged him down to the bedroom.

Chris glanced around at the horrible wallpaper and ugly brown carpet. "*Love* what you've done to the place," he said in a terrible falsetto, flopping both his wrists dramatically.

"Yeah, we'll get to it eventually, handyman."

With a grin, Chris walked across the room and sat on the bed. He bounced up and down a few times. "Mattress works."

"Hold that thought," said Dylan. He ducked into the bathroom and tried to remember where the hell he'd put the packet of condoms and bottle of lube, neither of which he'd used since the move. There were three cardboard boxes full of miscellaneous crap shoved in the corner—extra towels, a shower squeegee, soap dishes, things like that. He tossed these items everywhere as he burrowed in. Naturally, the two things he was looking for were in the bottom box underneath a half dozen spare boxes of Kleenex. Dylan made a small triumphant noise when the safe-sex paraphernalia were finally in his eager hands. He rushed back into the bedroom—but came to a full stop at the sight before him.

During the time Dylan had been in the bathroom, Chris had managed to strip off every thread of clothing. He was now splayed on his back atop the blankets, heavy-lidded, his legs spread wide and one hand lazily stroking his cock. His other hand was at his chest, the fingers tugging and pinching at an erect nipple.

He lifted one eyebrow at Dylan, who was still goggling. "You gonna fuck me, or what?"

Dylan dropped the stuff in his hands. He didn't bother to unbutton his shirt—he simply tugged it over his head, along with his T-shirt. He kicked off his Converses and fumbled at his belt, nearly tripping as he attempted to get his jeans and boxers off as quickly as possible. That left only his socks, which he tugged off impatiently.

Chris's eyes brightened as Dylan undressed, and he licked his bottom lip and smiled. "That's more like it."

After retrieving the lube and condoms from the floor, Dylan crossed to the bed. He desperately wanted to touch, but he spent a minute or two simply staring. Chris's shoulders were wide and his hips narrow. He had kanji characters tattooed on one calf. His muscles were solid and heavy, but as he shifted they moved fluidly beneath his skin, and his nipples were perfect brown peaks. He seemed to enjoy the admiration, because he stopped jacking himself and folded his arms beneath his head. The reddened crown of his cock dripped clear fluid onto his taut belly.

Dylan knelt between Chris's legs. He dragged his palms down the flat planes of his chest, across the ridges of his abs. Chris arched up slightly into the touch so that Dylan half expected him to start purring. He liked the way Chris's hair was flopping into his face, half screening his eyes. But then Dylan's gaze caught on the dark tufts of hair under Chris's arms. He leaned forward, blanketing Chris's body with his own, and nuzzled deeply at one armpit, filling his head with Chris's scent.

Suddenly smelling wasn't enough—he needed to taste. So he licked at smooth skin and wiry hairs. He traced his tongue down to a rib and then across, stopping to nibble slightly at one brown nub of flesh and then the other. Chris gasped a little at the pressure of teeth but didn't protest. He tasted good, Dylan decided. Warm and slightly salty, like bread fresh from the oven.

It turned out that Chris was ticklish—he wiggled slightly as Dylan worked his way down the center of his torso. But that was fine. Wiggling was good, especially when it made Chris's trapped cock slide against Dylan's chest.

Chris moaned and canted his hips upward when Dylan scooted down to lick at the tender crease between leg and body. But Dylan chuckled and pushed him back down. "Greedy," he said.

"Tease."

When Dylan urged Chris's thighs farther apart, the man obligingly bent his knees and folded his legs to his chest, leaving himself fully exposed. And that was exactly what Dylan had hoped for. With a happy little hum of approval he nosed deeply at the root of Chris's thick cock, at his heavy balls, at the tender bit of skin behind them. His head swam from the musky, sweet odors. He briefly wondered if it would be possible to come just from scent and taste alone. But then the thought reminded him that he could taste, and he did, lapping delicately at the perineum and then just at the edge of the tight little pucker.

"Jesus Christ! You're fuckin' killin' me, Dylan."

Oddly enough, although his own untouched cock was throbbing, Dylan was in no hurry. He smiled at Chris's groans and swearing, and he lapped and tickled around the rim of Chris's twitching hole. When he finally inserted his tongue, Chris let out a long, relieved, "Fuuuuck."

Chris's channel was smooth and silky against Dylan's tongue, and Chris was rocking slightly, trying to impale himself more deeply. Sweat had gathered under the folds of his knees. It slipped slowly down his thighs until Dylan raised his head and licked it away.

"If your dick is half as talented as your tongue…," Chris said with a laugh.

"Twice as talented." Dylan patted Chris's butt. "Roll over."

Chris was surprisingly willing to comply. He tucked his knees underneath himself and rested his shoulders on the mattress, raising his magnificent ass high in the air. Dylan spent a long time squeezing and rubbing and licking the muscular curves, then spread the cheeks and bent back down to tongue at—and in—the already moistened hole.

Soon Chris was rocking back and forth rhythmically, little huffs of air escaping noisily from his lungs. "Dyl... goddamn it... God... more!"

Dylan patted his ass again. "Ready for me?"

"Was ready half an hour ago."

Suddenly Dylan was ready too. He squirted a healthy dollop of lube onto two fingers but didn't bother to take his time inserting them slowly. Chris's ring of muscle was already relaxed. He jerked violently and grunted when Dylan deliberately scraped against the spongy little bundle of nerves. "Dylan...."

Dylan's hands were trembling slightly with excitement as he rolled the rubber onto his cock—the stimulation almost more than he could stand. When he lined himself up and sank inside in one slow thrust, both men moaned in unison.

"God, Chris. So tight."

"Been a while. You're—yeah, like that. God, just like that."

That was a long, gradual almost-withdrawal, followed by a quick slam back in. Dylan repeated the maneuver several more times, teasing them both, until Chris ordered, "Harder. Harder."

"Pushy bottom."

"Goddamn right."

Just when Dylan felt his balls drawing up tight, when he was in danger of losing himself completely, he stopped, producing an outraged wail from the man beneath him. "Don't!"

But Dylan wanted more. His skin was hungry for as much contact as possible. He ran his hands up Chris's spine and tugged at his shoulders until Chris was up on his knees in front of him. Chris's warm back against Dylan's front allowed him to reach around and wrap a hand around Chris's cock. Bucking forward into the grip, then back, Chris twisted an arm behind to grab at Dylan's torso. He let his head drop back onto Dylan's shoulder, and Dylan buried his nose in Chris's soft hair.

Skin slapped loudly against skin, punctuated by Chris's soft grunts and the thud of their heartbeats. Dylan rocked his hips and stroked with his hand. The sounds, the smells, the goddamn sublime *feel* of burying himself over and over again in Chris's hot core—his senses overwhelmed him, melding together until he couldn't tell them apart, couldn't distinguish which part of him was reacting to what part of Chris. He lost his rhythm completely and just pumped into that warmth until Chris cried out. The odor of Chris's semen was exactly enough to make Dylan fall apart. He gasped and threw back his head as he came.

It almost hurt to withdraw from Chris's body. As soon as he did, Chris collapsed onto his forearms with an *oof*. Dylan carefully removed the rubber and padded into the bathroom to throw it away. While he was in there he unearthed a couple of clean washcloths and dampened them at the sink. He didn't have the patience to wait for the water to get warm, but he knew Chris would be able to deal.

They cleaned themselves without comment. Dylan sat on the edge of the bed and watched as Chris pulled his clothes back on. "Want to come over for dinner?" Chris asked as he bent to tie his shoes.

"No thanks. I think I'll just have a sandwich or something."

Chris nodded and stood. His head was bowed a little so his hair hid his face. "I'll come over and help you unload the truck in the morning."

"Okay. But let's wait until Monday to paint. I have some work to get done."

"Suit yourself."

Chris turned and walked out the door. The shag carpet muffled his footsteps, but a few moments later Dylan heard the back door slam.

CHAPTER 10

DYLAN noted that for some unfathomable reason, Chris was in a foul mood. He wouldn't accept a cup of coffee, and he barely spoke as they unloaded the tile and supplies from the Chevy and carried them into the kitchen. When Dylan tried to begin conversations—when would the renter be plowing the fields? Did Chris ever trespass onto Dylan's land to fish down at the pond?—Chris's only response was an unintelligible grunt.

"See you Monday?" Dylan asked as Chris climbed into the cab.

Chris only glared at him, gunned the engine, and nearly ran over Dylan's foot as he pulled away. Judging by the sound of the truck, he didn't stop at his own place. Dylan wondered where he was going, then reminded himself it was none of his business.

He wandered back inside, where his laptop was waiting for him on his old drafting table in the living room. There was a big window that looked out at the field across the road, and he hoped that an eyeful of nature would prove inspiring as he designed the Beaverton house. But when his fingers started moving on the keyboard, he discovered that he was surfing online instead. Specifically, he was over on craigslist, looking at trucks for sale.

He found a few possibilities, and he made notes on them, wondering if Chris would be willing to tag along and check them out. Dylan knew nothing about cars except how to drive them. But perhaps he'd be wise to wait and ask when his neighbor was in a better mood.

He ambled into the kitchen, refilled his coffee mug, and grabbed a handful of sliced Diestel Ranch turkey from the fridge. He wolfed it down, wishing he could look forward to another of Chris's good meals later that day. Not to mention Chris himself.

Dylan sat back at his desk and spent twenty-five minutes rearranging his songs in iTunes and updating Adobe Reader and playing a game of solitaire.

"Okay," he said out loud when the cards did their rainbow dance across the screen. "Time to get to work."

So of course his phone rang.

"Farmer Dyldo!"

Dylan turned down the volume. His brother always seemed to think he had to bellow when he called. "Hey, Dickhead."

"How's it going?"

"Good. Busy. I have a new project—"

"It's Saturday. You're not supposed to work on Saturdays. It's un-American."

"The costs of working from home."

Something crashed in the background, and someone yelped. "What was that?" asked Dylan.

"Kay. She's rearranging the living room furniture. Again."

Dylan snickered. "Shouldn't you be helping her? Or at least checking to see if she's bleeding."

"The scream wasn't loud enough for a mortal injury, and I am helping her. She wanted me to call and tell you to come for dinner next time you're in town."

"Won't be for another two weeks."

"Aren't you—" There was another noise, this one even louder, and Dylan heard Kay swear. "Aren't you going nuts out there all by yourself?"

"Told you, I'm busy. I have that new project, and my kitchen's in ruins."

"Did you find someone to help out with the work?"

Dylan paused before replying. "Um… yeah."

"And why are you sounding hesitant?"

"It's my next-door neighbor, actually. He does good work but—"

"Wait! Is this the guy you saw pissing that time?"

Rolling your eyes was useless when you were on the phone, but Dylan did it anyway. "How many neighbors do I have, Dickhead?"

"So he does good work but… he doesn't know you're gay."

This time Dylan nearly choked. "No, he's well aware of my sexual orientation, thanks. I told you—it's been weeks since anyone was tarred and feathered out here for being queer."

"Then what's the problem?"

"Same as always." Dylan glared out at the field. "I'm worried about when I'm a wolf. What if I hurt him?" Saying it out loud like that made his stomach clench.

Rick thought for a while before he sighed. "I don't know what to tell you, little brother. If he's working for you, maybe you can send him away that night? Tell him… I dunno. Tell him you need him to get you something from Ashland that has to be transported overnight."

"He's not an idiot. He'd figure out something was up after a couple months. Besides, what the hell needs to be transported at night? Vampires?"

"Are there vampires too?" Rick sounded appalled.

"I don't know."

There was silence between them. Finally, Rick sighed again. "Sorry, kid. No easy solutions for you."

"Yeah. I know."

"So… dinner in two weeks, right?"

"Sure, Dickhead."

Dylan ended the call and stared at his screensaver. He'd managed to put aside his fears about Chris's safety for a few days, and now here they were again, front and center. "Well, cheer up," he told himself. "You'll probably have to move back to town anyway." And with that depressing thought he began work on the project.

HE SMELLED Chris before he heard him. At first he thought it was just wishful thinking, but then a familiar face appeared in the doorway. "Yo, dude. You should really lock your doors. Bad neighborhood, you know?"

Dylan pushed his chair back from the drafting table and stretched his arms. "Disreputable neighbors."

Chris entered the living room and looked over Dylan's shoulder. "What's that?"

"A laptop," Dylan answered with a grin, then ducked the playful blow that followed. "It's this new project I got handed the other day. Design a dream house for suburban hippie lesbian futon magnates."

"Oh." Chris blinked a few times. "So you really did have somethin' to do this weekend."

"Did you think I was lying?"

Chris shrugged and then stepped away to look out the window. "He's probably gonna plow next week. You'll know it when he gets here—crack of dawn."

"Okay." Dylan stood and stared at Chris's back, wishing he could reach out and put his hand on a flannel-clad shoulder.

"And yeah, I used to go fishin' down there. Caught tadpoles, too, and sometimes I even went swimmin'. I wasn't supposed to, but I figured the old man wasn't gonna care. He didn't leave the house that often." He set his hands on the windowsill. "Sometimes if I sat real still, deer would come by for a drink."

If Dylan's ears had been capable of pricking at that minute, they would have. His stomach rumbled. "Deer?"

"Sure. I saw otters a couple times too."

Dylan wondered what otters tasted like.

Chris spun around quickly and pointed at the laptop. "Can you leave it for a while?"

"Yeah. I was planning to shut down pretty soon anyway. Why? Are you making us dinner?" Dylan was aware that he sounded foolishly hopeful.

Sure enough, Chris laughed. "Not exactly. We're goin' out for a night on the town, dude."

THE "town" wasn't much of one: a gas station with a few mechanics' bays in the back and a little general store next door; a feed store; a place that sold pizza, burgers, and ice cream; a little building that housed a real estate office and a lawyer. But at the end of what amounted to downtown was a big gray structure with several cars and motorcycles parked in the adjacent gravel lot. Chris pulled the Chevy in between a beat-up Harley and a rusted Ford truck with a gun rack.

"What's this?" Dylan asked, not sure whether he was pleased.

But Chris flashed him a grin. "Saturday night."

Before they left the house, Dylan had put on a shirt that didn't say anything ironic. Now he was kind of wishing he'd shaved off the soul patch too. The patrons of Buck's Café and Tavern wore denim skirts and tight blouses if they were female, jeans and T-shirts and John Deere hats if they were male. Men had mullets or brush cuts, and women wore their hair… puffy. Activity in the tavern didn't exactly screech to a halt as he and Chris entered, but Dylan could sense everyone eyeing him, sizing him up.

"I'm not sure this is such a great idea," Dylan said. But Chris apparently didn't hear him over the sound of the jukebox. Instead, he led the way to a booth near the back. The wooden tabletop was sticky. He pushed at Dylan's shoulder until Dylan was sitting.

"I'm gonna go get us beer and grub," Chris almost shouted. "Burger okay?"

"Yeah."

As Chris made his way to the bar, Dylan looked around. The tavern was crowded enough that he wondered if the entire town showed up on Saturday nights. The décor was minimal—mostly rough-planked walls and neon signs advertising beer. A space to one side was free of tables and had a small stage, but there was no sign of a band. The air was heavy with the smells of frying food, stale beer, cheap perfume, and sweat. Dylan realized he was wrinkling his nose and forced himself to relax.

It didn't take long for Chris to reappear with two glass tankards. A little foam sloshed over the edges when he set them down. "Food'll be up soon," he said, taking a seat opposite Dylan. "It ain't all that great, but it's the only game in town."

"Do you come here a lot?"

Chris lifted an eyebrow. "You tryin' to pick me up, dude?"

"This doesn't exactly look like a good place for picking up guys."

"Mostly it ain't." Chris took a long swallow of beer. "But you'd be surprised what some of these good old boys get up to in the john, when they get enough alcohol in 'em and the gals ain't willin'."

Dylan was not the kind of guy who entertained fantasies about straight men. Even the thought of trying to do anything with one of the bikers or other burly men in the room made him feel slightly queasy. He wondered if his sarcastic comments to Rick about people around here no longer gay bashing for sport were going to come back to haunt him.

His thoughts were interrupted when a man with a dark beard and mustache, head wrapped in a blue bandanna, approached the table carrying two plates. The man plopped them on the table, then added the ketchup and mustard bottles he had tucked under one arm. Without having said a word, he turned and went back to the bar.

"Least that dude ain't tryin' to jump your bones," Chris muttered.

The burger wasn't that great: the meat was gristly and overcooked, the lettuce wilted, and the bun tasted like a sponge. The fries were pretty good, though, and Dylan managed to keep Chris from stealing any of his.

"I practically grew up in places like this," Chris said, waving his hand around. "When I was really little—after Dad left—Mom would sit me down at a table with a hamburger, maybe a coloring book and some crayons, and tell me to sit tight. Some nights I'd fall asleep in a booth like this one. If I was lucky I'd wake up in my own bed."

Dylan didn't know how to respond. Surely Chris didn't want trite sympathy. "That sucks," he finally said.

"How 'bout you? No horrible childhood in the 'burbs?"

"No, sorry. It was boring. I spent a lot of time in my room, reading. My parents kind of freaked when they found out I was gay, but that wasn't until I was older."

"What, did they disown you or something? Were they religious freaks?"

Dylan glanced at a petite redhead making out with a guy with a graying ponytail. "No. They were just pretty conservative. They were… disappointed. I was still living with them, but after they found out, we hardly saw each other, hardly ever talked. Maybe they would have thawed if they'd had more time to adjust."

"They didn't kick you out?" Chris asked, puzzled.

"No. I was in college, working at a coffee place to pay for tuition and books. I couldn't have afforded a place of my own."

"So they loved you, even though you were a homo."

"Yeah. I guess they did." Dylan had never really thought about it, and the realization that his parents really did love him eased an ache he hadn't known he had.

Chris gave Dylan his half grin and slammed his empty glass on the table. "Want another?"

"No, but you go ahead." As Chris walked back to the bar, Dylan formulated a plan to confiscate the keys to the truck before they left. There weren't a lot of other cars to run into between here and home, but there were a lot of trees.

A crowd had formed around the bar, so Chris had to wait a while. Dylan finished off his dinner, wiped his mouth with a paper napkin from the dispenser on the table, and looked around. That's when he noticed two men sitting at a table in the middle of the room. They were only a few years older than he and Chris but looked as if they had lived a lot in those years. One of them was fat, with a shaved head and a vivid scar across his cheek, and the other was jittery, bouncing up and down nervously in his seat. They both had their eyes on Chris, who either hadn't noticed them or didn't care. Although he didn't even glance at them as he made his way back to their booth, they tracked him the entire way.

"I got you a Coke," Chris said as he sat. "Diet, so you can keep your girlish figure."

"I'm pretty sure you know there isn't much girlish about my figure, Chris."

Chris waggled his eyebrows. "You got a point."

They sat there for a while, talking a little but mostly just watching the action. Dylan had to admit that it was kind of nice being out of the house. But he was also worried about the way those men kept eyeing Chris.

Suddenly Chris stood and slammed his palm on the table. "Be right back." He walked to the dimly lit back of the tavern and turned down a hallway that Dylan assumed led to the bathrooms. That reminded Dylan of Chris's earlier comment about good old boys and johns, which worried him. That concern increased several notches when the pair got up from their table and sauntered down the hall as well. Their timing could be a coincidence, he told himself, but he didn't really figure these guys for the type who went to the bathroom in packs, like girls, or the momentary lovers who visited the bathroom at Bleachers.

"Shit," he said out loud. And he headed for the hallway too.

He heard the raised voices while he was still several yards from the men's room, but the relentless twang and boom of the jukebox kept him from being able to distinguish the words. One of the voices was Chris's, though—of that he was certain—and his heart raced in distress even as he ran the last few steps.

The door was locked. Dylan pounded on it a few times but got no response. The voices inside sounded angry, and he heard a loud thump. He briefly considered running back to the main room for help, but he didn't know whether anyone would be willing. And in any case, who knew what could happen in the few minutes he was gone. He could call the police, but that would take even longer—the nearest police station was many miles away.

He banged his fist against the door three more times and then, for good measure, kicked the door twice. "Fuck off!" yelled someone inside. There was another cry as well, muffled as if the person were gagged somehow. That one sounded like Chris.

With adrenaline pumping through his veins and his pulse thudding in his ears, Dylan kicked with all his might, just next to the doorknob. Luckily, this was not a steel door like the one in his old pantry. The wood splintered and buckled. He kicked one more time, and that was enough to pop the latch right out of the frame. As the door swung open, he charged inside.

Chris was down on his knees, facing the big man. At the crash of the door, he turned his head, and Dylan saw that his right eye was swelling closed and a trickle of blood dripped down his chin. The huge guy had been holding him in place and, rapidly, his enormous hand clamped tight over Chris's mouth. The jittery guy had been facing the other two but swung around to look at Dylan. He had a pocket knife in his hand, blade extended.

"Let him go!" Dylan shouted.

But the big guy didn't release his grip, and the smaller man only gave a thin-lipped smile. "You want a turn with Chrissy too, sweetheart? His mouth is real nice. Or maybe you wanna help your girlfriend out and take his place?"

Dylan watched as the rivulet of blood trickled lower, onto Chris's chest. The eye that wasn't swollen shut was wide with fear. Dylan should have been afraid too, but instead, red rage engulfed him. "Get your fucking hands off him!"

The big guy snorted and twisted Chris's head back toward his groin, while the other man took a step closer to Dylan. The point of the knife was roughly even with Dylan's stomach.

For a bright hot moment, Dylan knew what their flesh would taste like in his mouth. He longed for the delicious feel of skin and muscle tearing and the satisfaction of gnashing at tendon and bone. He growled, low and deep, and he bared his teeth. "Go. Away."

He had no idea what the men in the bathroom saw when they looked at him. But the close guy went very pale, dropped the knife, and darted past Dylan and into the hall. The big guy let go of Chris and seemed to hesitate for a second, so Dylan growled again, louder this time. "Please don't!" the man yelped, and Dylan's nose was filled with the harsh scent of urine as the guy pissed himself.

Chris scrambled to his feet. His gaze stayed firmly on Dylan's face.

But Dylan just stood there, his fingers curved into the semblance of claws and his entire body quivering with need. He wanted hot blood spurting down his throat, and he wanted to bury his face in warm entrails.

"Dyl?" Chris said, very quietly.

That broke the spell. Dylan stepped aside, and the big man lumbered past him. He was in such a hurry that he bashed into the door frame and bounced off like a big rubber ball. But Dylan paid no attention. He walked the few feet to Chris and started to reach toward the injured eye but stopped himself. Instead he let his hands settle on Chris's shoulders. "Are you okay?"

Chris licked the trickle of blood from his lips. "You were gonna kill those guys." His voice was soft and flat.

"They were hurting you," was all Dylan could say in response.

Chris opened his mouth as if to say something and then shut it. He shook his head. "Let's... let's get the hell out of here."

That was an excellent plan, Dylan thought. He followed Chris past the ruined door and down the hallway, away from the tavern's main room. At the end of the corridor, they went through a grimy door marked with an exit sign and found themselves behind the tavern, in a weedy area littered with broken bottles and other debris. Chris stopped and looked around as if he were considering his options.

"We need to call the cops," Dylan said.

"Don't bother. Those assholes are long gone, and what's the point? Ain't like the deputies are gonna care anyway."

"They hurt you!"

Chris wiped the back of his hand across his mouth. "I'm fine." Then he looked back at Dylan. There was something wary in his gaze, as if he were debating whether to run.

"You knew those guys," Dylan said.

Chris shrugged and turned away. "Long time ago. Wouldn't've come if I knew they'd be here." He took a few steps into the darkness, his feet crunching softly on the gravel. And then he turned again. "What the hell was that back there, Dylan? You were scary as hell."

"I...." Dylan swallowed thickly. "I didn't want them to hurt you, okay?"

"But you almost... Christ, Dylan. I thought you were just this quiet kinda guy, really hot but sorta... meek. You ain't that guy, are you?"

"I used to be."

Chris cocked his head to the side and advanced to within a few inches of Dylan. "You could've killed those guys. I saw it in your eyes." He huffed out a small laugh. "So did they. Is that why you moved out here, Dylan? Did you... hurt someone?"

"No!" Dylan replied. But he remembered the thick smell of blood and the screams of mortal terror, and he knew his answer wasn't quite the truth. "Almost."

"And you scared yourself, didn't you? So you moved away from people 'cause you figured that'd be safer."

Dylan nodded dumbly. He was wondering how he'd get home after Chris abandoned him in this parking lot. There weren't any taxis for sixty miles. He could probably call Rick, but that would end in long, uncomfortable explanations. Hell, he might as well start walking now.

He turned and took a step or so toward the road, but Chris caught his sleeve. "You stood up for me when those fuckers…." He took a deep breath and let it out. "I guess you're disgusted with me now."

That wasn't at all the response Dylan had expected, and he blinked in surprise. "No! Jesus, no, Chris."

Chris's shoulders slumped a little in relief. "You can't get away from your past, man. You know? You think it's been long enough or far enough… but it ain't. Never is." And then his lip curled in that half smile, charming even when the lip was puffy and split. "So you're some kinda homicidal maniac, and I used to be a bigger whore than my mom. Guess those are a couple secrets we both wish had stayed buried."

"I'm sorry."

Chris moved closer until their chests were almost touching. He reached up and grabbed a handful of Dylan's hair. "I ain't never had nobody rescue me before," he said.

"I've never rescued anyone before."

Dylan expected Chris to kiss him then, and in fact, Chris did bring his face forward until their lips were nearly touching. But then he abruptly moved away again. He grabbed the elbow of Dylan's jacket and tugged. "Come with me."

Privately, Dylan was thinking they'd already had enough adventure for the evening. He was ready to head back home. Maybe Chris would invite him over to watch some TV for a while. Maybe he could persuade Chris to let him put some ice on that eye. But when Chris led him away from the parking lot and toward a dilapidated old storage shed, Dylan didn't resist.

It was dark and silent behind the shed. Dylan's night vision had improved after he was bitten, but even still, he could only make out Chris's outline, punctuated by the slight glint of his teeth and uninjured eye. Dylan didn't know what the other man could want back here, but then Chris pushed him back against the shed's corrugated metal side, and Dylan understood. Still, he was taken aback when Chris gave a quick kiss to the corner of his mouth, dropped to his knees, and started fumbling with Dylan's belt.

Dylan batted Chris's hands away. "Hey. You don't have to."

Chris stood and punched the wall beside him. The resulting boom startled Dylan, but he didn't move. "You think that's what this is?" Chris snarled. "Think I'm payin' you off for savin' my ass?" He was standing close enough for Dylan to feel his breath, and for a moment Dylan thought Chris might hit him next.

But Chris didn't swing again. He simply stood there, breathing hard, until Dylan gently wrapped Chris's fist in his palms and lowered his arm. "You're going to hurt your hand too."

Chris slumped against him, so that for a few seconds Dylan bore all his weight. It was kind of nice, although Dylan didn't quite dare to wrap his arms around that solid body. "You were fuckin' hot," Chris whispered. "Staring those fuckwads down like a real badass. Like goddamn Clint Eastwood or somethin'."

Dylan snickered. "Clint Eastwood?"

"What? You're more of a John Wayne kinda guy?"

Dylan was formulating an answer, but he never got a chance to say it because Chris was suddenly back on his knees again, and Dylan's fly was undone. Dylan gasped at the rare sensation of cool air on his dick, but before he could pull away, his cock was slipping neatly between Chris's enflamed lips, and cold was replaced by moist heat.

"Chris!" Dylan choked out. He wasn't sure what he meant by it, but Chris took it as encouragement, sucking gently and fondling Dylan's balls with his rough fingertips.

Dylan had never been a big fan of public sex, and the last time he'd had sex outdoors was on a two-night camping trip with Ery Phillips during his junior year in college. It had rained the entire time, and neither of them could get the campfire lit. Plus, somehow it seemed that their parts didn't quite fit together, and the fucking had been mediocre at best.

There was nothing mediocre about the blow job Dylan was getting from Chris.

Dylan put his hands on Chris's shoulders, partly for balance and partly to ground himself a little, because Chris was pressing his tongue against his frenulum, and Dylan's brain felt like it might float up into the clouds. Then Chris withdrew just a bit and scraped the edges of his teeth against Dylan's glans. Not enough to hurt, but plenty to cause pleasurable bolts of fire to run up Dylan's spine.

"Jesus, Chris. That's... Jesus!" He lost the ability to form words. His knees threatened to give, and his head bashed noisily against the wall, but when Chris opened his throat and swallowed him down, Dylan could only moan.

Above the soft sounds Chris was making, Dylan's sensitive hearing could make out faint noises from the tavern—voices and music—and in the other direction, insects chirping and small creatures scuttling through leaves. Somewhere very far away an owl was calling.

He wanted to warn Chris, he really did. It was the gentlemanly thing to do, right? But if he said something then that incredible feeling around his dick might stop, and Dylan didn't want that. Besides, he didn't seem to be able to make his mouth work properly. He clutched Chris's heavy shirt in his fist and fought to keep from bucking forward. Chris bobbed his head and stroked behind Dylan's balls, and that was it. When Dylan climaxed, he smacked his head into the wall again, this time hard enough that he literally saw stars.

Chris stood up and kissed him again. Dylan moaned as he tasted himself on Chris's tongue. But apparently tucking himself back in and buttoning up was his own problem, because Chris turned and walked toward the parking lot. With a shake to clear his head, Dylan hurried to catch up.

CHAPTER 11

THE next two weeks zoomed by. The cabinets would be ready soon, so during the day Dylan and Chris painted and tiled. Even though Chris continued to cook for him, Dylan was looking forward to having a working kitchen of his own. Sometimes they'd screw after dinner, perched on Chris's ugly couch or sprawled on his bed. But then Dylan would slog back to his own place and slave away on the Beaverton project.

Chris had been right: the farmer started work very early.

The hippie clients were getting an oversized Craftsman bungalow, Dylan decided. Cedar siding that would weather beautifully, a wide front porch that could house a crowd of futon-cushioned lounge furniture, and a huge master bath with skylights and a whirlpool tub. Also two guest bedrooms, a great room with dog-friendly hardwood floors, and a dog door in one wall of the kitchen. Nice, comfortable, and classic. Like Birkenstock sandals, he thought.

The morning before Dylan was supposed to meet with the clients, he greeted Chris with a wide grin. "How about something different today?"

Chris gave him a skeptical look. "Whaddaya have in mind?"

"Car shopping. Well, truck."

This time, Chris's expression was inscrutable, but Dylan thought surprise flickered across those blue eyes. "Okay," Chris said.

Truck shopping ended up taking all day. First they drove to St.

Helens to take a look at a Toyota, but Chris said the payload was too small for Dylan's needs, and it wouldn't be able to tow a big enough trailer. Then they crossed the river and checked out a Dodge Ram. Dylan didn't say so, but he thought the truck was really pretty, with shining red paint and gleaming chrome. But when they took it for a drive Chris said it wasn't driving straight. "Could be bad alignment, but I'm bettin' on a bent frame," he said. "This baby was in a wreck."

A little discouraged, Dylan took them through downtown Portland, stopping for lunch at the sandwich place where he and Matty had gone.

Chris was trying to say something with his mouth chock full of smoked turkey, avocado, and bacon. He chewed a few more times and swallowed. "Man, this is good! Only time I get bread like this is when I make it myself."

"You make bread?"

"Ain't that hard," Chris said with a slight blush under his dark skin. He looked adorable, and Dylan had to squelch an impulse to lean across the table and kiss him. *He's not your goddamn boyfriend*, he reminded himself sternly.

For dessert, Dylan took them to Voodoo Doughnuts, which turned out to be somewhat of a religious experience for Chris. "Holy shit! They have a maple bar with bacon! And a chocolate doughnut with Butterfinger. And… fuckin' A! That one's got Oreos and peanut butter." But the one shaped like a cock and balls—with Bavarian cream filling—made him laugh so hard that the lady in line ahead of them turned and frowned. Dylan bought them a baker's dozen, and Chris tenderly carried the pink box back to the Prius.

The sugar raised both their spirits considerably. Chris bounced happily in his seat, but Dylan had to fight hard to keep his eyes on the road when Chris sucked the frosting off his own fingers.

A dealership in Hillsboro had a used Silverado. Its silver paint sported a few scratches and dings, but Chris nodded approvingly at the vehicle. "You can tow almost eighteen thousand pounds," enthused the barrel-chested salesman. Then he started talking about torque and steering knuckles, and Dylan sort of tuned out. Chris popped the hood and spent some time poking around, after which they took it for a drive.

"Well?" Dylan asked as they pulled back into the lot.

"It'll do. They're askin' way too much, though. Don't pay more than twenty grand."

"And how much do you think I can get for a trade-in on the Prius?"

Dylan tilted his head. "You're really serious about this."

"Well, yeah. I'm not quite ready to haunt the John Deere dealership, but I need something more suited for farm life."

"What about when you move back to the city?"

"You still think I'm gonna throw in the towel?" Dylan was a little shaken by Chris's lack of confidence in him.

"You ain't... you ain't.... Someone like you can't be happy out in the middle of fucking nowhere."

"It's not like we live on Mars, Chris."

Chris looked away. "Might as well," he muttered.

"Look. When I first saw you I figured you were a homophobic, dimwitted redneck. The kind of guy who pisses off his back porch. And now I know you're none of that. Except the pissing part."

"I was kinda wasted."

"I figured. I've noticed since then that you're fully capable of using indoor plumbing. So if I can get past my assumptions about you, can't you do the same for me?"

Finally making eye contact again, Chris said, "I thought you were one of those hipster assholes who says he wants to grow his own food but faints dead away the first time he realizes there ain't no artisan falafel in the entire county."

Dylan smiled slightly. "I hate falafel."

The salesman had been hovering under the broad awning of the dealership building, no doubt thinking they were debating the purchase.

When Chris opened the truck door and slid to the pavement, the salesman came trotting over. "So, whatta ya think? Pretty sweet, huh?"

Dylan joined Chris, who frowned. "I don't know. Ford F-250's got a bigger payload and more horsepower."

"Yeah, but this baby's got an Allison transmission and independent front suspension. Our customer satisfaction blows them out of the water. And—" He glanced at Dylan and then back at Chris. "—this one'll run on B20 biodiesel."

Chris negotiated the deal. While Dylan was inside signing paperwork and writing checks, Chris stayed in the parking lot and transferred all of Dylan's belongings from the Prius to the truck—especially the remaining doughnuts.

POMEGRANATE and Cassidy McMaster-Evans smelled strongly of patchouli and chamomile. Pomegranate's gray hair was buzzed close to her skull, whereas Cassidy's was waist length and still mostly blonde. Their clothing was made of hemp with, he guessed, natural dyes. They were both smiling at him expectantly across the conference room table.

"We're so excited to see what you've come up with!" Cassidy exclaimed. She had a beautiful, melodious voice, like a radio announcer. Her partner nodded enthusiastically.

Dylan felt slightly nauseated. He'd filled an insulated cup with coffee before he left the house, and when he hit the city limits he'd done drive-through for a refill, so now his stomach was sloshing uncomfortably, and he was a little lightheaded. He cleared his throat and rubbed the back of his neck. Matty poked his leg under the table—hard—and Stender folded his hands serenely in front of him.

"Um... I... I didn't have a whole lot to go by in the files," Dylan stammered. "Usually it's good—uh, usually I like to meet with clients before I begin."

Cassidy leaned forward. "But we didn't want to interfere with your creative energies. We just wanted everything to flow naturally—"

"—from the creative wellspring," Stender finished for her.

"Exactly. Too much intensity early on, too many different forces mixing together, and everything gets cloudy. Like dipping paintbrushes in water."

Dylan had a sudden and vivid mental image of Chris's reaction to hearing a conversation like this, and he had to bite his lip to suppress a nervous snicker. "Well, I tried. But, you know, if you don't like stuff of course we can change things."

There was a slight pause, during which Dylan found himself desperately wishing he were back in his own dismantled kitchen, listening to Chris sing badly and replacing the fluorescent light fixture in the ceiling with those nice pendants he'd brought home the other day.

"Dylan? Why don't you show us the plans," his boss prompted.

"Uh, yeah. Sorry." Dylan flipped open his laptop and keyed in his password. When the file booted up, he turned the screen around so the clients could see. "So, um, here's the front elevation. I'm going to suggest we place the house fairly far back on the lot. Not enough so you don't have a backyard, of course, but enough to give a little more privacy. We can curve the driveway a little too, so you have a little more sense of drama as you enter the property."

He risked a glance at the clients. The McMaster-Evanses were peering intently at the computer—Pomegranate had put on a pair of reading glasses—but their expressions remained fairly neutral.

"I've gone with a side-gabled bungalow because I think it gives the house more visual depth, more interest. That gives us this nice deep porch too. I used cedar shake here, but we could also mix in some stone if you wanted. I have a source for some nice reclaimed limestone. I've sketched in some four-over-one sash windows. The house won't be too out of place in the neighborhood, but it'll still be distinctive."

Everyone stared at the screen, and nobody said anything. After a moment, Dylan cleared his throat and pressed a button to reveal the first story floor plan. "We're going for a great room concept here. We can talk a little more about what you're looking for in a kitchen, but for now you can see it's nice and open, with a couple of exposed beams in the living area. I was thinking reclaimed wood for the walls—sort of a cabin-in-the-woods feel—or maybe we could stick to drywall but do one wall in stone."

He went on like that for what seemed like hours. Nobody interrupted him as he described the plans and explained some of the options. The clients exchanged a few glances with one another, which he couldn't read, but mostly they looked at the computer. Sometimes one of them nodded.

"And, um, I guess that's it," he said at last. Although he was relieved to finish, the knot in his stomach remained.

The silence was very heavy. Pomegranate removed her glasses and tucked them into a case, which she put in the small embroidered bag that hung across her chest. She and Cassidy locked eyes so hard and for so long that he began to wonder if they were capable of telepathy. Dylan jiggled his leg, realized what he was doing, and stopped. Matty poked him again. And Stender looked as if he was meditating on the phenomenology of being.

"It's nice," Cassidy finally said.

Pomegranate nodded. "Very pretty. And that fancy dog door— that's a nice touch."

Silence fell again. Dylan suddenly became aware that he had to pee really, really bad. Finally, Stender unfolded his hands and smiled serenely. "If you're pleased with what Dylan's given us so far, we can schedule another meeting for next week. We'll be able to hammer out a few of the details and get some cost estimates."

The women looked at each other again and then at Dylan. "It's very nice," Cassidy repeated, and Dylan's heart sank. "But it's not... I'm sure it would be lovely for someone else."

For the first time, Matty stepped in. "Is it the materials that bother you? 'Cause those are super easy to switch out. Or maybe you'd like some more traditional room spaces...."

"It's not that, dear." Cassidy patted Matty's hand. "We were hoping… well, we were hoping to make a statement, I suppose. Other than 'We have tons of money' or 'We have impeccable traditional taste.'"

How about "We spent a little too much time eating 'shrooms," Dylan thought. What he said was, "I'm not sure what you mean."

Cassidy sat up very straight in her seat. Her fingers played with the collar of her muddy green blouse, then stilled. "It's about irony. The introduction of the exotic into a mundane setting."

"The house still has to be livable, of course," Pomegranate added.

Her partner smiled and nodded. "And we don't want to be run out of Beaverton on a rail. But we don't want to live in the same house as everyone else, no matter how nice it is."

Dylan hung his head. If someone had clued him in on all this to begin with, he could have created something completely different. He could have saved his job.

"I'm sorry we didn't meet your expectations," Stender said. He didn't sound especially upset, and his smooth face was unworried.

Cassidy said, "I'm sure Dylan tried very hard. The energies just weren't right. Sometimes the Goddess is with us, and sometimes she has other plans." She leaned forward, placing both her palms on the smooth wood of the tabletop, and looked intently into Dylan's eyes. "You seem like such an earnest young man. I bet you work very hard."

"I… I do."

"It's not all about hard work all the time, honey. You need to sit back sometimes and let the powers flow through you. Stop worrying about being… prudent. Be brave! Go wild a little!" Her laugh was like tinkling bells. "If Pom and I had gone the safe route we'd probably still be selling our futons at Saturday Market and living out of our Vanagon."

"Uh… thanks," Dylan said, because he couldn't think how else to respond.

"Would you rather I turn the project over to someone else?" asked Stender, and Dylan ducked his head again.

But Pomegranate tsked. "No! We'd like to give Dylan another stab at it. He'll come through. I know he will."

Dylan lifted his head and gave her a grateful smile. "Thank you." But relieved as he was to be given a second chance, he had a terrible feeling that it was only a temporary stay of execution.

CHAPTER 12

MATTY was sympathetic and comforting and supportive all at once, patting his back and chirping assurances until his head hurt and he feared he might snap at her. Stender said very little. After the clients left, he steepled his hands again and inclined his head toward Dylan's laptop. "You'll be on it right away, I take it?"

"Of course."

"Your remodeling won't get in the way?"

"This project will be my first priority."

At that, Stender nodded and stood, then sailed out of the conference room and back to his office. Dylan wanted to bang his head on the table, but Matty was still there, blabbing on about creativity exercises and removing the barriers to the flow experience.

"I gotta go," Dylan said, a little abruptly. He stood and snapped his laptop shut and scooped it under his arm.

"Are you sure? We could have a drink or something. Heck, we can have a bunch of drinks. If you get too buzzed to drive home you can always crash at my place. My couch is free."

"Thanks, Matt. But I have a dinner date."

Her eyebrows raised. "Date?"

"Just Rick and Kay."

"Oh," she said, disappointed. "Dyl, I don't know how you're ever gonna meet—"

"Not this again. Please. Not now, okay? I really have to go."

She made a face that reminded him of the one his mother had made when she was disappointed in him. But she stepped out of his way and watched silently as he left the room.

Probably nobody else in the office gave a damn about his presentation, but still, he felt as if every eye was on him as he made his way down the hall and, heavens be praised, to the men's room. A minute or two later, he was forced to tolerate an instrumental version of "Come As You Are" playing in the elevator. He had used a parking garage a block and a half away, and he kept his head down as he dodged other people on the sidewalk heading home from work. He was so preoccupied with his own failure that he nearly got run over by a light rail train as he crossed the street, and then a bicyclist rang her bell and cursed at him as she zoomed by.

He trudged up the stairs to the garage's third floor. For a moment he was lost and a little confused because he couldn't find his familiar green Prius, but then he remembered that the big gas-guzzling monster at the end of the row was his. "Stupid," he mumbled to himself. He unlocked the truck and went first to the passenger side, tossing in his laptop bag and the big accordion folder of various papers Stender had handed over to him. He slammed the door shut, but before he went around to the driver's side he paused and pulled his phone from his pocket. He really wasn't up for socializing. He'd call Rick and beg off, promise to reschedule the following week or the week after. Hopefully Kay wouldn't be too pissed off.

"Given up on going green?"

Dylan spun around so quickly that his phone slipped from his hands and went flying, shattering into pieces on the concrete floor.

"Wow. That's a shame. Sorry about that," Andy said, stepping out from the shadow between two SUVs. He was grinning delightedly.

"What the fuck are you doing here?" Dylan cringed at the way his voice shook.

"You didn't want to talk to me last time. I was hoping maybe you'd change your mind if we were on neutral territory. Come on. We can go have a couple of drinks—"

"I told you I didn't want to see you again."

"Of course you were gonna say that, with your boyfriend standing there."

"He's just my neighbor."

Andy's smile didn't dim as he prowled a few steps closer. "You sure about that, Dyl? I can practically smell him on you."

"It's none of your goddamn business."

"Hey, it's okay. He's pretty tasty. We can add him to the pack if you want." Andy licked his lips. "He'd make a nice little omega, wouldn't he?"

Dylan's fists were so tight that his nails were digging into his palms. His eyes darted from side to side, but he didn't see anything he could use as a weapon, and he was pretty sure he couldn't make it into the truck before Andy got to him. He could shout for help, but it was doubtful that anyone would hear—and even if someone did, he didn't want to place an unsuspecting stranger in the middle of this. He didn't know how much damage Andy could inflict in human form, but based on the strength Dylan had experienced in the tavern bathroom and on the way his muscles were bunched and ready right now, Dylan felt fairly certain that either of them was fully capable of killing a human with his bare hands. And teeth. God, Dylan wanted to bite.

He took three deep breaths and let them out. Maybe if he stayed calm he could make Andy just go away. But it was so hard to keep his cool around Andy. Just the sight of him sent Dylan's emotions into overdrive. "What is it you want?" he said as calmly as he could.

Andy's smile turned up a few notches, and he came even closer. Dylan had to fight the urge to back up against the truck. "I'm glad you're finally ready to listen, man." Andy was so sexy: his curls just a little too long, his brown eyes clear and bright, his heavy muscles visible under his tight clothing. Even the bulge at his crotch was clearly outlined. "Let's go have those drinks. And maybe something to eat. I'm starved."

"Just spit it out."

"Okay," Andy said with a shrug. "This thing with you and me—it was an accident, right? I didn't mean to hurt you that night. I was trying to get out of the house, but sometimes it hits so quick— Anyway, I didn't mean to make you like me."

"Is that what this is all about? You're trying to apologize—like a 12-step program for the supernatural?"

Andy shook his head and held out his hands, palms up. "No, man. I'm just trying to explain. I didn't plan any of it—I've never been all that great at planning—but it happened, and we gotta deal."

"You mean *I* have to deal. That's what I've been doing, Andy, and I don't need your help."

For a moment, Andy appeared wounded, but then his easy smile reappeared. "Yeah, you got your Green Acres and everything. But you're all by yourself, Dyl. Humans aren't supposed to be alone, and neither are wolves. You need a pack, man. You need me."

Dylan would have liked to call him a liar, but at least part of what Andy said was so true that Dylan's heart clenched. Almost gently, Dylan said, "I do need someone. But you're not that someone. I'm sorry."

Andy's handsome face twisted into a snarl. "I fucking *made* you! You might not remember what a loser you were before, but I do. All this"—he waved a hand in Dylan's direction—"it's my doing. That piece of ass out in the boonies, he wouldn't have even looked at you before."

"Maybe so," Dylan replied evenly. "But that doesn't change the fact that I don't want you. I can't. Not after—" His words choked off, and he looked away, his jaw working.

"That's what we are, Dylan. You can sit there all day and pretend you're this... this sophisticated man who has a fancy job and a Facebook page and GPS in his fucking truck, but that's not what you are. You're a predator, baby. Like me."

"I'm not like you." Dylan hoped he sounded more convinced than he felt. "Why are you so stuck on me anyway? You said it yourself—I was an accident. Go find someone else."

"You think I haven't fucked anyone since you? You think your ass is so sweet I can't look at anyone else?" Andy cupped his hand over his dick. "Let me tell you, baby, that ain't no problem."

"Jesus, Andy, are you even listening? If you're getting laid all the time, then what's the obsession with me?"

"It's not the same!" Andy roared, then seemed to try to control himself. "It's not the fucking I need. I told you—it's... it's family. *Pack.*"

Slowly, Dylan shook his head. "Not me. I'm not your pack. There must be someone else."

A dark look came over Andy's face, and Dylan's stomach lurched as he realized exactly what was coming. Andy shook his head and in a low voice said, "I tried. I *tried*, man. But none of them.... They didn't make it. That's not what I meant to do, but once I change, once I smell them and I taste them...."

Dylan shuddered. How many others had there been before him, and after? How many men who didn't have a steel door to hide behind when the wolf appeared? He felt like he might be sick. But Andy reached for him with one hand, almost but not quite touching him. "You don't know, Dyl. Don't know what it's like.... It's been a lot longer for me than for you. You'll see. After a while it just eats at you, this fucking need. Like hunger, right? I found... a couple years back, I found some others like us. I tried to run with them for a little while, but it wasn't the same. They weren't mine."

"I'm not—"

"Try it! Give that hillbilly a little nibble when the moon is full, and you'll see what I mean."

For a moment, Dylan could picture it clearly: his sharp teeth sinking into tan skin, hot, sweet blood filling his mouth. And then Chris would be his. No need any longer to run alone, no need to hide what he was, no more of this ever-present fear of hurting someone he cared about. Except... what if he went too far when he bit? What if he did to Chris what Andy had done to countless others? And even if he didn't, even if he could somehow maintain enough control to stop himself, then he would be responsible for turning a good man into a monster. Just like him.

"I don't belong to you, Andy, and I never will. Get out of my fucking life."

Andy's face went red with rage, and Dylan was positive that the man was going to go for his throat. But just then a car alarm beeped twice, startling them both, and they turned to see a man in a suit standing near one of the SUVs. The man had his key fob in one hand and his phone in the other, and he was staring at them, wide-eyed.

Andy turned back to Dylan with a silent snarl, panting heavily. "You'll see, baby," he growled. "You'll see." Then he spun around and ran for the stairs.

Dylan slumped against the tailgate and tried to slow his racing pulse.

"Hey! Are you okay?" That was the man in the suit, still keeping his distance but with his thumb hovering over the touchscreen of his phone.

"Yeah. Thanks. He's just… never mind. Thanks."

"I can call the cops."

"No, it's okay. I'm gonna leave anyway."

The man looked slightly doubtful, but he nodded and got into his SUV. Dylan watched as one of the tires ran over the remains of his phone. With a heavy sigh and slightly shaking hands, Dylan opened the truck's door and climbed inside.

He was now even less in a mood to have dinner with Rick and Kay, but he had no way to call them and didn't want them to worry. He was slightly embarrassed to realize he didn't even know their phone numbers—he usually just pressed a button in his contacts. So he exited the garage and made his way across downtown and onto the freeway. Halfway there, though, he was overtaken by such severe shaking that he had to take the nearest exit and pull to the side of the road. He turned off the engine and spent a few minutes breathing deeply, trying to calm himself. When that didn't work, he closed his eyes and tried to imagine himself somewhere peaceful: on his own front porch, sweaty and sore after a day's good work, Chris leaning beside him and smoking, clouds scudding over the newly tilled fields across the road.

But without willing it and before he could stop it, that tranquil scene was replaced by a very different one. He was in the living room of his old house, four weeks after Andy had disappeared. The wounds on his leg had healed, leaving pinkish indented scars, but that fall evening they were itching nonetheless. He felt as if he were buzzed on caffeine, as if he were waiting for some important event, and his T-shirt and shorts felt tight and restrictive. He'd noticed the way his muscles had grown over the past weeks. People at work kept asking him about his new exercise regimen and telling him he looked great. Men on the street and in restaurants were making eye contact with him, looking at him with hope instead of disinterest. He'd had to buy new clothes. He wasn't stupid, and some part of him knew what all this signified, but another part refused to believe. Who the fuck believed in werewolves?

Just before sunset, when Dylan was pacing the room as restlessly as a caged animal, a knock had sounded on the door. When he opened it, Andy came barreling in, hair in wild snarls, eyes gleaming with a feral light. "Get out of here!" Dylan had yelled and tried to push him away.

But Andy was bigger and stronger, and he'd folded his arms around Dylan's body, holding him tight. "Hang on, baby," he had rasped in Dylan's ear. "You're in for a ride."

Dylan hadn't struggled, and within minutes he'd felt the unnatural bending and stretching and tearing that had later become so familiar, the fundamental restructuring of a human body into something smaller, stronger, faster. He had writhed and shrieked on the living room floor in front of his gaping suburban front door, and when the change was finished he had howled his grief and hunger and excitement.

He had followed the other wolf—his alpha—out into the night. The neighbors had already gone indoors, but if any of them had glanced out a window they likely would have assumed that they saw a pair of big dogs. Shepherd mixes, maybe. They might have considered calling animal control but then decided to make dinner instead.

Andy and Dylan had loped for a mile or two until they came to a greenbelt that ran along a creek and smelled of a thousand people, of their dogs and their children, of discarded food wrappers and cigarette butts and ancient wads of chewing gum. The mixture was intoxicating. Dylan's mouth hung open, and his tongue lolled out as he ran. The blacktop was slightly rough on the pads of his paws.

And then Andy had banged his shoulder into Dylan's and yipped softly. They ran full out, faster than Dylan had ever moved without a vehicle. It felt fucking wonderful, all that speed at his command, his legs so powerful. He now realized he'd been slow and weak all his life, nearly deaf, hardly able to smell. How had he managed?

He didn't know how long they ran. Time had become nearly meaningless, anyway. There was a bit of Before and a hint of Later, but mostly there was a whole lot of Now.

Dylan had fallen slightly behind when Andy picked up a particular scent and bayed at him to hurry up. Dylan barked back and followed his alpha away from the greenbelt, down a quiet street where plastic toys littered front yards and a For Sale sign squeaked quietly in the breeze.

A cat darted out from some bushes, and Dylan leaped after it until Andy growled at him. Somewhat reluctantly, Dylan rejoined his companion on a sidewalk that still retained some of the day's warmth. They ran onward three blocks, then four, and that's when Dylan realized what scent they were following. It was very fresh, no more than a minute or two old, and it was human.

They turned a corner, and Dylan saw him up ahead: a jogger with his earbuds playing tinnily, his shoes slapping rhythmically on the ground. He smelled good—sweat and youth—and as he ran Dylan found himself irresistibly drawn to chase. The man didn't yet hear them and was too oblivious to notice, but he was prey.

It didn't take long to catch up to him. Dylan thought Andy would leap on him from behind, and he readied his muscles to do the same, but instead Andy ran ahead and circled around, blocking the jogger's way. The jogger yelped with shock and skidded to a halt. "Hey! Hey, shoo!"

Andy raised his hackles and growled.

"Uh… good dog. Nice dog. I'm just gonna…." The man tried to back away and nearly tripped over Dylan. "Oh, fuck!"

The wolves circled the man, who now reeked of fear, a scent that made saliva pool in Dylan's mouth and drip from the corner of his lips.

"Help!" the man suddenly shouted. "Somebody help me! I'm being attacked!" Nobody opened their front doors to look, and no people appeared at front windows. Maybe nobody could hear the man over the babble of their televisions. But the man screamed again anyway. "Help me! Call 911!"

Dylan had retained enough of himself to be amused. What the hell good did this guy think calling the cops would do? By the time the patrol rolled up there'd be little left of him but bones and gristle.

Maybe the man realized that as well because he shut up. He swiveled his head from side to side and then rushed past Dylan, dashing headlong at the nearest house. He never got there, of course. The wolves outpaced him easily and cut him off. Andy huffed softly, and Dylan knew that his alpha was only playing with the guy, working him up a little just for the fun of it. But then somewhere a few blocks away a dog began to bark. Andy's stance grew tenser, more businesslike. He growled again, a deep rumbling in his chest, his head held low and his sharp teeth showing.

"Oh no, God, no, please." The jogger's distress had made him all the more delicious. Dylan longed to bite, but he wouldn't, not yet, not until his alpha signaled that he should.

And then Andy had swung his head to the side slightly to make eye contact with him, yellow eyes meeting yellow eyes glowing eerily with something wild and ferocious. No longer men, but something straight out of a million horror movies. A couple of monsters.

Andy barked once more, sharply, and then leaped. The jogger was borne to the ground. The acrid scent of urine filled the air and then, just a split second later, the rich salty odor of blood. The man couldn't even scream. He gurgled and batted weakly at the wolf upon him, but only for a moment. Then he was still, and Andy was burying his sharp muzzle inside the man. Dylan licked his lips, took a cautious step forward—and then turned and ran.

If Andy had chased him then, he probably would have caught him. Andy was much stronger, more accustomed to this form. And he was alpha. But Andy was too occupied with his kill to bother. So Dylan ran home as fast as he could, and when he got there he ran through his still-open door and jumped up to push it shut behind him. A wolf couldn't manage a doorknob, but Andy could still smash through a window, so Dylan had again taken refuge in the pantry, pushing closed the salvaged steel door.

In the cold light of the morning, with Andy gone, Dylan had considered calling the police. But what could he tell them? If he talked about werewolves he'd end up in a loony bin at best, in some kind of... research facility at worst. Instead, he had done nothing except call in sick and spend the day reading and rereading the accounts of the dog attack, the horror and self-loathing periodically forcing him into the bathroom to puke.

The next day he transferred the reinforced door from the pantry to his spare bedroom and the monthly lock-in began.

CHAPTER 13

DYLAN took another sip from the glass etched with a twirly mustache and smiled at his sister-in-law. "Thanks for dinner, Kay. It was great." She'd made lasagna, which she knew was one of his favorites.

Kay curled her legs under herself on the couch. "What've you been eating out there anyway?"

"It's not the end of the world, Kay. They have food."

"Roots and berries?" she asked with a grin. "C'mon, Dyl. You don't look like you're wasting away, but I know there's no drive-through."

"I'm not completely helpless, you know."

"Not completely. But you don't have a kitchen, and even if you did, a guy can only live off grilled cheese and nuked pizza for so long."

With a sinking feeling in his gut, Dylan realized he'd walked into a trap. Kay had claimed they couldn't possibly eat the pie she'd baked without ice cream and then feigned surprise when she discovered that someone had eaten the last of the Dreyer's. But that had clearly been a ploy to get Rick out of the house so she would have Dylan all to herself. He wondered if she had written all her questions down ahead of time so she wouldn't forget any of them. "I kind of have... um... an arrangement going," he mumbled.

That was the wrong way to say it; he could see that immediately. Kay's thin eyebrows flew up, and her green eyes went round. "An arrangement?"

He stared down desperately at his lemonade, but it wasn't helpful at all. "It's… my neighbor. Chris."

"The guy who's helping you with the remodel."

"Right. And it turns out he likes to cook, and since he's right next door, well, it kind of made sense."

"You're paying him to be your chef?"

Why hadn't he just told her he was living off sandwiches? "Not exactly. But we split the grocery costs, and he doesn't mind. He says it's not any more work to cook for two."

She looked at him so sharply that he had a deep stab of sympathy for the child she and Rick were trying so hard to conceive. Poor kid was never going to get away with anything. But then she must have decided to move on to the next item on her list, because she shifted slightly, rearranged a pillow, and set her lemonade glass atop a coaster on the coffee table. "Are you okay, Dylan?" she asked. "You look kind of beat."

He looked, he figured, like a guy who had been shot down at work, accosted by a homicidal ex-boyfriend in a parking garage, and tortured by visions of murder and cowardice during his evening commute. "It's been a long day," he said.

"Is the commute getting to you?"

"No, that's okay. My truck's pretty comfy. It even has an mp3 jack." Which was pretty useless until he got another iPhone, he remembered. But Kay looked like she was waiting for more details. He decided to fill her in on the easier part of his problems. "The clients didn't like the plans I presented today."

"No way! You do such good work! Bastards." She looked slightly outraged on his behalf, which made him smile. Yes, occasionally time with Kay made him thankful for being gay—he didn't understand how Rick could live with such intensity and such constant talk about *feelings*—but she accepted him with all his flaws and had even become his fierce advocate.

"They just wanted something different," he explained, and then described that afternoon's scene at the office.

When he was done, Kay tapped her front tooth thoughtfully with a fingernail. "I can see where the futon queens were coming from, maybe. Your houses are beautiful. But they're kind of... safe, aren't they? Safe as houses." She giggled. "Safe's a good thing, Dylan, but sometimes you have to color outside the lines."

He was still thinking about her words and trying to formulate a reply when the door from the garage slammed shut. Rick entered a moment later with a paper bag in his hand. "This better be really good pie," he said.

Kay unfolded herself from the couch and walked across the room so she could grab the sack away. "Never question my pie, honey." She gave Rick a loud smooch on the cheek. "While I'm warming it up you can get Dylan to spill about his new squeeze."

Dylan sputtered and almost choked on his lemonade. Rick shrugged and took Kay's spot on the couch. "New squeeze?"

"Traitor!"

"Let's face it, little brother. My allegiances have shifted. If it comes down to you or the little woman, she's gonna win every time. And not just 'cause I'm sleeping with her."

"I heard that!" Kay called from the kitchen, and Rick made a *See what I mean* face.

"So... who's the lucky guy?" Rick asked. "Or, you know, sheep."

Dylan suppressed the urge to stick out his tongue. "Hah. Besides, it's goats we have the hots for in Columbia County."

"Tell him or you don't get any pie," yelled Kay. That was a scary threat, because her pie was really good.

Dylan sighed. "I don't have a... a... someone. I was just telling Kay that Chris has been sharing his dinners."

"'Sharing his dinners.' Is that some kind of gay euphemism that I don't really want defined?" asked Rick with a smirk.

"No, Dickhead. It means the same for us as it means for you breeders. Chris cooks food, like noodles and chicken and stuff, and we eat it. That's it. Because I don't have a kitchen."

Rick picked up Kay's lemonade glass and drained it in one long swallow. "Chris is a pretty handy guy to have around, isn't he?"

"So?"

"Nothing. Just saying."

Dylan glared at his brother silently, and Rick picked up the remote control and clicked on the TV. That gave them both the excuse to stare at the screen as Rick scrolled through the guide. After a few seconds he put on *The Daily Show*. They listened as Jon Stewart interviewed some guy who wrote a book about foreign policy. The guy was pretty funny, Dylan thought, and he wondered if they practiced the banter ahead of time. He briefly imagined himself sitting in the guest's chair, laughing with Jon Stewart about the funny aspects of being a werewolf. Not that there were too many of those.

"You are a pair of idiots," Kay announced when she returned to the living room. She was carrying a tray decorated with green and yellow cartoon owls. Dylan took one pie-filled plate off the tray and Rick took another. Kay set down the tray and squeezed between the brothers, her own plate and fork firmly in hand.

Dylan didn't usually have much of a sweet tooth, but there was no way not to love boysenberries and cream cheese with a healthy scoop of vanilla bean ice cream melting over the top. "Oh my God," Dylan moaned with his mouth full. "Why are you in HR and not a baker?"

"'Cause I'd weigh five hundred pounds if I was around goodies all the time." She grabbed the remote off Rick's leg and turned off the TV. "I wanna hear about this Chris guy."

"Why? He's just... just a guy."

Kay eyed Dylan's plate like she might be considering taking it away, so he clutched it possessively and shoveled a huge forkful into his mouth. "You have a thing for him," she said firmly.

"I do not!"

"Every time I bring him up you get this little fuzzy look in those big hazel eyes of yours."

"I don't—There's no fuzzy!" Dylan looked at his brother for

backup, but Rick only grinned and shrugged. No rescue there. "He's....
We kind of spend a lot of time together 'cause it's just the two of us out
there, and we've been doing all that work together. So I guess... yeah, I
guess we're friends."

Until he said those words, Dylan had been assuming that Chris
was a fuck buddy and a coworker, but that was all. Now he knew that
the assumption was wrong—Chris really was his friend. Someone
whom he enjoyed hanging out with even when they weren't screwing
or laying tile. He liked Chris's sarcastic sense of humor, the way he
liked to tease. He liked the way Chris could wear his country rube
persona so comfortably and yet surprise with his little digs and offhand
comments that reminded Dylan that Chris was actually a very
intelligent man. And then there was the way he was so generous with
his time and energy—he only took a paycheck when Dylan insisted,
and for much less than he was worth—and so good-natured about
Dylan's various issues. Dylan also admired how Chris didn't wallow in
self-pity or seethe in anger over his crappy upbringing or the
difficulties he'd had as a young adult. And he was so goddamn sexy
with his crooked smile and clear blue eyes and his tan skin, so soft over
hard muscles, and....

Dylan looked at Kay's triumphant face. He felt as if he'd been
bashed over the head with a sledgehammer like a cartoon coyote.

"Told you," Kay said.

The delicious pie suddenly tasted like sawdust, and Dylan had to
struggle to swallow the rest down. Still feeling in a daze, he accepted a
stack of Tupperwared leftovers, thanked Kay and Rick, and stumbled to
his truck.

CHAPTER 14

"I THOUGHT you were gonna do the upstairs first," Chris said, peering uncertainly into the half bath on the ground floor.

"Change of plans." Dylan had indeed planned to tackle the master bath first, but that would have meant spending the day with Chris very close to his bed. Up until last night, Chris near his bed—or, better yet, Chris *in* his bed—would have seemed like an excellent idea, albeit counterproductive to remodeling progress. But today Dylan was still trying to absorb the previous night's realization, a process that was not going well. He would have begged off doing any work at all and just sent Chris home, except that would have raised questions he couldn't truthfully answer.

Chris seemed oblivious to the turmoil in Dylan's head. "If we rip this out you ain't gonna have any water at all on this floor until the kitchen sink and shit get here. Gonna be a pain in the ass when you want to clean up after work or wash out your coffee cups."

"I'll survive."

Chris looked at him a moment and then shrugged. "Whatever, dude."

Dylan pushed past him into the little room and knelt to begin unscrewing the bolts that fastened the toilet in place.

They worked mostly in silence, first removing the fixtures, then peeling away the vinyl floor. Dylan had decided on the spur of the moment that if they were going to be redoing this bathroom first, he might as well add a shower stall. That required enlarging the room itself, so while Chris scraped glue off the floor, Dylan dismantled one of the walls.

"Hey, dude. What's up?"

Dylan had his head down as he tried to pull a piece of stubborn lumber free. He looked over at Chris, who was stretching out a kink in his back. "What do you mean?" Dylan asked. His voice sounded odd through the mask he was wearing.

"Dunno. You've been kinda... off all morning. Like you got somethin' on your mind."

What didn't Dylan have on his mind? He felt as though his brain was like his old Prius, normally practical and efficient but currently weighed down by a much too heavy load. He sighed and hoped the mask hid his guilty expression. "The meeting yesterday didn't go well."

"That sucks, dude. But hey, you can't please everyone, right?"

"My boss has made it pretty clear that if I fuck up this project he's going to nix the whole telecommuting deal."

For a brief moment, a look of pure panic flashed across Chris's face. Then he seemed to regain control of himself. "So you'll redo the plans."

"I don't... I don't know if I can do it."

"Sure you can. Just hit delete. Even I can do that." The corner of Chris's lip twisted up slightly.

"And then I have to come up with something new. Something ironic and exotic yet livable and not too objectionable to the neighbors. How the hell am I supposed to do that?"

"I dunno, dude," Chris said quietly. "But I'd bet the farm that you'll pull it off."

Dylan didn't know what to do in the face of such confidence. Couldn't Chris tell that he was nothing but a loser who knew how to run a drafting program? Nothing but a boring guy from the 'burbs who had always faded into the background until the fringe benefits of being a monster kicked in. Dylan shook his head and went back to that stuck piece of wood.

By one thirty the bathroom was completely pulled apart. Dylan was about to suggest they call it a day—maybe he'd take the opportunity to go buy a new phone—when they were both startled by a knock at the front door. "Who the hell is that?" Dylan asked.

"Your house, dude."

Dylan stripped off his mask and gloves and dropped them on the floor. He picked up his hammer, though. If Andy showed up he probably wouldn't announce himself so obviously, but Dylan wanted to be sure. Chris trailed along behind him.

Maybe Dylan should have been relieved when he saw that it was Kay at the door, but instead he felt his stomach tighten with anxiety. He let her in anyway, of course, and she enveloped him in a tight hug. Over her shoulder, he could see Chris frowning.

When Kay pulled away and Dylan could breathe again, he said, "What are you doing here? Is everything all right?"

"Everything's fine. I haven't seen the farm yet, and you weren't answering your phone, so I thought I'd come inspect."

"Oh. Um, I dropped it yesterday. It broke."

"What is it, a genetic thing? Rick's been through, like, four of them this year." She walked around him and stuck out her hand. "Hi. I'm Kay."

As Dylan blushed at his lack of introductions, Chris's scowl was replaced by a bright smile. "The goddess who made that incredible pie." He shook her hand. "Chris. Dylan's neighbor and hired hand. And finally I get to meet a relative. I was beginning to wonder if he'd been raised by wolves." Chris looked at both of them in puzzlement as they burst into laughter. Dylan's had a hysterical tinge. "Didn't realize I was that funny," Chris said mildly.

"Sorry," replied Kay, shooting Dylan a quick but evil glare. "It's kind of a family in-joke. So. I hear you've been keeping my brother-in-law from starving to death."

"Been tryin'. I don't make killer pie, though."

She smiled at him. "Dyl's more of a meat kind of guy anyway." Dylan wanted to strangle her.

Chris, on the other hand, seemed delighted with Kay, and for an uneasy few seconds Dylan worried about how he was going to manage them together. But then Chris said, "We just finished destroying shit. I'm gonna head home. Get Dylan to give you the grand tour."

"You bet. It's nice to meet you, Chris."

"Same here." Chris whacked Dylan on the back as he walked by. "I got pork chops tonight if you want 'em, dude."

"Um, yeah, thanks."

As soon as Chris was gone, Kay began to bounce on the balls of her feet. "Oh my God, Dyl, he's delicious!" He blushed, opened his mouth and shut it, and turned his head away. She didn't seem to mind, because she grabbed his hand. "C'mon. Show me the homestead."

"Okay."

He had to admit, it was kind of fun to show the place off to someone—even in the poor shape it was in—and listen to her ooh and ah. He should have known she would be capable of seeing the potential in the place, of seeing the solid structure and nice little details, of ignoring the ugliness and appreciating what the house could be. Good bones, Steve the Realtor had said, and that was it exactly.

"Do you know how you're going to furnish it?" she asked when she'd seen all the rooms.

"Maybe. I'm usually not an antiquey kind of guy, but too much modern just isn't going to look right. I think maybe I'll mix them up a little. Mostly new stuff, but enough old to fit in."

"Perfect!" She clapped her hands and bounced again. "I know! My grandma had all this great stuff, but when she went into that assisted living place she gave it to us. We can't really use it, but I didn't want to get rid of it, so we rented a storage locker. Let me know when you're ready, and you can take a look. It'd be nice to know some of her stuff was being used."

"Thanks, Kay. That'd be great." Then he had an idea. "If you want, you guys can haul it all over here and store it in the basement. You saw for yourself—there's plenty of room, and I don't own much. Save you the storage fees."

She leaned up to kiss his cheek. "We'll pay you in pies." Then she walked to the front window and looked outside. "Want to show me the estate? It's pretty decent out."

She was right. It was a little muddy but warm enough that he didn't need his jacket. It was really beginning to feel like spring. He knew there were plenty more days of cold and gray left until they reached the few coveted days of summer sunshine, but this was a pleasant tease. He showed her the pump house and the little barn, which he planned to convert to a garage and workshop eventually. Then they walked down the slightly slick path to the pond. "Chris says I'm going to need to clear the blackberries once or twice a year if I ever want to get down to the water again," he said. "I'm going to have to learn to drive a tractor."

He could see her casting a glance at him from the corner of her eye. "Chris is a helpful guy, isn't he?"

Dylan sighed. "Did you really drive all the way out here just so you could get a look at him?"

That made her punch him in the bicep. "Dope. I came because I was worried. Meeting him was a bonus."

"Worried?"

By then they were at the bottom of the slope, and they stood there silently for several minutes while she took in the scene. Everything was lush and green already, and even in his present form Dylan could catch the scents of a myriad of creatures small and large—including deer and elk. He didn't think he'd be able to take one down on his own, but he'd enjoy tracking it, and besides, there were plenty of more manageable prey.

"This is amazing," breathed Kay. "I can't believe you actually own it. We could have campouts here."

"You guys bring the s'mores."

She put her arm around his waist and squeezed. "This is good, Dyl. I think you made the right choice."

He sighed. "So why are you worried?"

"'Cause last night you looked like someone dropped a bomb in your lap. Why is it so traumatic that you're finally falling for someone? He seems like a great guy. And cute."

He pulled away from her embrace and stood with his back to her, looking out toward the forest. "I can't... I can't do it. I can't fall for anyone."

"So, what? You're gonna spend your whole life alone? Dylan, what happened to you isn't your fault. Stop punish—"

He whirled around "It *is* my fault! If I hadn't been stupid enough to take Andy home with me... I saw his pretty face, and I was so thrilled he wanted *me* that I didn't even think. So goddamn stupid!"

She came closer to him and enveloped him in a hug. "Honey, how the hell were you supposed to know he was a werewolf?" She gave him a little squeeze and then took a half step back, keeping a hand on his shoulder. "You know, girls grow up knowing they should be careful of strange men." She gave a small laugh. "Beware of the big bad wolf, right? But guys, nobody tells you that. You don't think that way, like you might be vulnerable. Not even if you're dating other men. You pretty much figure as long as you use a rubber you're safe."

"Maybe," he said, not quite willing to concede that she was right. "But it's all beside the point, anyway. It happened, and now I'm screwed. Or not, as the case may be."

Her mouth pursed as she thought. "Dyl, what.... Does Chris think you two have something serious going on?"

"No. It's not like that with us. I think I'm just convenient."

"And that's why he looked so relieved when he found out I'm family?" She shook her head a few times. "I bet he's as gone as you. Men. Would it kill you to actually *talk* to each other for once?" Her tone was both fond and exasperated.

"Kay, even if I told him that I lo—that I care about him, then what? I can't tell him I'm a fucking werewolf."

"Why not?"

He blinked at her. "Why not? Can you just picture that conversation?"

"You had it with us," she replied calmly. "You sat us down and you told us what happened. And, well, we kind of freaked I guess, because who expects to hear that? But we got over it."

"You had to," he said miserably. "You're family."

"If he cares about you he'll deal too. He'll know that you're smart and sweet and kind and creative and sorta dorky and totally hot, and he'll deal with the wolf thing. It's like my friend Holly. I've known her since seventh grade, and I love her so much that I can overlook the fact that she votes Republican. What's a little monthly furriness compared to that?"

A pair of mallards appeared over the treetops and splashed onto the other side of the pond. They immediately started shaking their tails and submerging their heads, and Dylan realized he was licking his lips. "I'll hurt him," he said in a near whisper.

"That's a risk everyone takes when they fall in love. Besides, I don't see you as the love 'em and leave 'em type."

He shook his head. "No, I mean I'll literally *hurt* him. I'll kill him."

"If he knows, he can protect himself. It's only one day a month."

"So now he's the poor bastard who has to lock himself in a reinforced room? Or leave his home altogether?"

Kay watched the ducks for a minute or two, then turned back to Dylan. "Tell him, sweetie. He's worth the risk."

Dylan shook his head. He couldn't. He should probably just throw in the towel right now and move back to town. He could get a restraining order on Andy and spend the rest of his life safely locked away every twenty-eighth day. If just imagining that scenario—

picturing himself leaving Chris and abandoning his freedom—made him feel ill, how the hell would he manage to live it?

"Let's head back to the house," he said to Kay. "I've got this delicious leftover lasagna for lunch."

CHAPTER 15

CHRIS and Dylan eased the stove into place, taking care that it was perfectly located between the hickory cabinets. Then they stood back and looked around. "It looks fuckin' amazing," Chris said.

Dylan nodded slowly. "It's hard to believe we did this all ourselves."

"Wait 'til you get the whole place done, man." Chris bit his lip for a moment. "Unless you're thinkin' it's time to head back to the city."

"I *told* you. I'm here until my boss gives me an ultimatum, and then... then I guess I'll figure something out."

Chris took a rag from the island and used it to wipe at a small spot on the stainless steel refrigerator. "Then you'll go back," he said with his back to Dylan.

"I don't know. I could live off my savings for maybe a year, but then I'd be flat broke."

"But you'd have a place to live." Chris turned around and tossed the rag back onto the counter but still didn't make eye contact. "Could do like me, play it by ear, find a job when you need one."

"I can't do that, Chris."

"Yeah. I figured. It's beneath you, with your fancy college degree and all. You ain't a backwoods hick like me."

Dylan sighed and wished he had the balls to walk across the room and force Chris into an embrace. He'd been thinking that way a lot lately—wanting to not just fuck him but to hold him, to murmur stupid things in his ear. But he couldn't. Intimacies like that would be lies, promises he'd have to break. And in any case Chris would probably be horrified that Dylan was making this into more than a casual fling.

"It's not beneath me," Dylan said, "and yeah, you're rural but definitely not a yokel. I just can't live loose and easy. The uncertainty, you know? I need a safety net."

"You got family you could go to if shit happened."

"Rick and Kay would pull me out of a bind, but I wouldn't want to do that to them. They don't have all that much extra to give, and they're trying to have kids."

"Friends, then."

"Nobody I could rely on."

Chris's face went very blank, and he stomped over to the sink to wash his hands. "You done with me for the day?" he growled over the sound of the water.

"Um… I was thinking maybe we could go pick out the stuff for the bathroom."

Chris turned back to look at him. "We?"

"Sure. Unless you're busy. We could take the flatbed and load up. I think I'm going to buy off-the-shelf for this room."

There was a blue and white dish towel next to the sink, but Chris dried his hands on the legs of his overalls. The motion reminded Dylan of how nice those thigh muscles felt under his hands, how thick and strong they were, how good they looked when Chris was bent nearly double with his thighs almost framing his face. He swallowed loudly.

"All right," said Chris. "Let's go."

The flatbed's seats were as hard and unforgiving as milk crates and transmitted every bounce and jostle on the road. The windshield wipers squealed asthmatically. The cab reeked of old engine, and if Chris turned on the heat the air vents smelled like something had crawled in and died. But the truck ran fine, and it could handle loads that were too big even for Dylan's pickup. Besides, Dylan thought there was something incredibly sexy about the way Chris looked while he drove the big vehicle. Chris's sleeves were rolled above his elbows, revealing the ropy muscles of his forearms, and he was wearing a baseball cap pulled low on his head—maybe to hide the speckles of paint that had landed in his hair during the morning's touch-up job. He had apparently gotten over whatever was making him angry earlier, because he was humming little snatches of songs, and sometimes he'd glance over at Dylan and smile.

Dylan wondered how uncomfortable it would be to have sex on top of the bench seat.

They ended up driving all the way into the city to a huge plumbing supply place frequented by a lot of the contractors Dylan knew. The place carried a good range of products from cheapo to *holy shit*. Dylan concentrated his efforts on some of the nicer midrange fixtures. He ended up choosing a large pedestal sink with an antique reproduction faucet, and a frameless glass shower enclosure. He was going more for function than historical accuracy in this room, although some of the planned detail work would assure it didn't end up totally anachronistic. After he picked out a couple of light fixtures, a towel bar, and a mirror, Dylan found Chris near the back of the store, seemingly enraptured by an enormous bathtub.

"You could host a pool party in that thing, dude."

Dylan frowned at it skeptically. "My water pressure's only so-so. It'd take a year to fill it."

"I know," Chris said with a disappointed little sigh. "But a girl can dream."

Dylan was pretty familiar by now with Chris's single bathroom: a tiny space with a cracked Formica countertop over a particleboard vanity, a chipped mirror, a toilet that made alarming sounds when it was flushed, and a slightly mildewy plastic shower compartment. "You know, my master bath's still in rough shape, but the tub's pretty nice. You can use it anytime you want."

Chris seemed surprised by the offer. "Yeah?"

"Sure."

A slight curl of the lips. "Might take you up on that. I bet you got some of them smelly things too—salts or oils or some shit like that."

"Are you casting aspersions on my masculinity?"

Ignoring the nearby pair of men in coveralls, Chris leered hugely. "Wanna go home and prove what a man you are?"

With the bathroom supplies secured onto the flatbed, they next stopped at Lowe's, where Dylan bought some floor tile and paint. The bathroom would still need something for storage, but he was thinking that later on he'd hunt for an old shelf or something, a piece with a little character to offset the minimalist shower.

"Between today and the kitchen stuff, you've put a good dent in your budget," Chris observed as they headed out of town.

"Yeah, but I'm still good. The only other really pricey part's going to be the master bath. The rest is mostly paint and hard work." He took a long sip of the coffee he'd picked up at the Starbucks near Lowe's. "For upstairs I was thinking I might use some real antique fixtures. There's this place near downtown. They specialize in salvaged stuff."

Chris nodded but didn't say anything. Either the traffic was taking a lot more concentration than usual or he was deep in thought. Finally, he cleared his throat. "I been thinking."

"Oh?" Dylan wasn't at all sure he was going to want to hear this.

"You got that big-ass kitchen, all shiny like somethin' from a magazine, and you ain't hardly gonna use it. And I got my old place and… and maybe sometimes I could come over and cook us dinner. If you want."

Between the kitchen and the bathtub, it sounded as if Chris was practically going to move in with him. Hell, they already spent most of their waking hours together, working on Dylan's place, eating and then watching TV at Chris's, and fucking in both houses on a variety of surfaces. Despite knowing that he should be more careful, that all of this was bound to end badly, Dylan couldn't help but smile as his heart beat fast with delight. "You can come over and cook for me any day, Chris. Every day, even."

Chris cut his eyes briefly to the right and then looked back at the road. "What about when you got a guy over?"

"A guy?"

"Yeah. A… a date."

Dylan was momentarily so flabbergasted that he didn't know how to respond. He could see the way Chris's mouth had tightened, though, the way his shoulders seemed suddenly very tense. He remembered what Kay had said about Chris thinking more of him than just convenience. Maybe she was right. She usually was, according to Rick.

"I won't have any dates over," Dylan said quietly.

"Right. You probably take 'em somewhere in the city. Not to a Podunk tavern where shitheads get jumped in the men's room."

"No, I mean I won't have any dates, period. I don't have anyone in my life. Just… just you." Goddamn it—they were having a relationship talk in the slow lane of Sunset Highway.

Chris shook his head. "I seen the way guys look at you—even the ones that've been fooling themselves they ain't interested in men. You could have half'a Portland dropping trou and bendin' over for you."

"Um… I think that's overstating it. And anyway, I won't. I'm not seeing anyone else, Chris."

Now it was Chris's turn to look shocked, so Dylan hastily added, "I'm not saying you have to… that we have… that I'm stopping you from… whatever. I mean, we can… Jesus, Chris. I suck at this."

But Chris was smiling. "You sayin' you're gonna gimme your class ring and let me wear your letterman jacket?"

"I didn't play any sports in school."

"Built like you are?"

Dylan blushed. "I was a… late bloomer. And now you're changing the subject. Look." He took a deep breath. "There are things about me—bad things. And I can't, I can't… it won't work long term. I won't blame you if you don't want to… to be with me anymore, or if you want to look for the guy you really deserve. But I'm not going to have sex with anyone else."

Chris's expression was troubled, but he nodded slightly and cracked his window a little to defog the interior. Dylan didn't know what else to say, and it seemed the discussion was over because Chris just stared at the taillights in front of them.

WHEN they first arrived back at the farm, it was as if the entire conversation in the truck had never taken place. Chris was very businesslike as he helped Dylan unload the purchases and stow them in the living room. When that job was complete, Chris stood in the kitchen, running his fingers through his hair. "Seems a shame to dirty it up already. Wanna come over for dinner?"

Dylan should have been working on the Beaverton project. He'd done nothing but stare at a blank screen and reject every lame idea that sprang into his head. But he probably wasn't going to be successful tonight anyway, and there was something strangely vulnerable about the way Chris was holding himself: a sort of resigned wariness to his eyes and a little hunch to his broad shoulders. "Sounds good," Dylan said, earning a bright smile.

Dinner turned out to be thick steaks and potatoes baked just right, with crispy skins and the insides moist and soft. There were fresh chives—which Chris grudgingly admitted he'd grown himself—and a spinach salad, and big bowls of ice cream for dessert. "Kind of a feast," Dylan said, rubbing his happily overstuffed belly.

Chris just gave his half smile. "You get to wash the dishes while I sit on my ass and watch."

That was fair enough, and they chatted lightly as Dylan cleaned. They heard the wind rushing through the treetops and agreed that a storm was on the way. Chris had a tractor among his vehicle collection—not quite running, of course—but he thought he could get it going by the time Dylan needed it to clear blackberries.

Usually after a meal like that they'd both collapse on Chris's ugly couch and argue good-naturedly over what to watch on TV until they ended up naked. But tonight Chris stood in the middle of his small living room, shifting slightly from foot to foot. Finally, he said, "Were you serious about that bathtub offer? 'Cause it sounded pretty good."

Dylan smiled. "Dead serious. Come on over."

It had begun raining, hard, and they were soaked by the time they re-entered Dylan's kitchen. But they didn't pause to do more than kick off their boots—"You oughtta add a mudroom back here," Chris advised—before heading upstairs. As Dylan stripped off his wet clothes, Chris entered the bathroom. The sound of running water followed almost immediately.

"Let it run a while," Dylan called. "Hot takes forever." He pulled on a pair of gray sweatpants and a ratty old T-shirt and sat on his bed, imagining Chris just on the other side of the wall, wet and naked. After a while, however, it occurred to him that he could do more than imagine. He stood and padded across the room, pausing at the bathroom threshold to peek inside through the open door.

What he saw took his breath away. Chris was lying in the tub, his eyes closed and his head tipped back against the rim with a folded towel as a pillow. The heat of the water made his dark cheeks slightly ruddy, and a few tendrils of hair stuck to his skin. He must have found the gift basket of Kay's homemade bath items—another of her craft projects. The humid air smelled strongly of lemon and spices, and the water was slightly cloudy with oil. But Dylan still had a clear view of his lover's submerged body, of the dark curls that slightly floated at his groin, of his cock lying soft and thick against one thigh.

"This feels like fuckin' heaven," Chris said, without opening his eyes.

"It's a big tub." God, sometimes Dylan wished he could bite off his own tongue to save himself from being terminally lame.

But Chris's mouth curled into a slight smile. "Wanna join me?"

"I don't think it's that big."

"In the room, dope. Have a seat and keep me company. It's better than lurkin' in doorways."

Dylan was going to sit on top of the closed toilet, but then he decided he wanted to be nearer to Chris, so he sat on the floor instead, his back against the wall and his arm leaning up against the tub. Chris was facing him, but his eyes were still closed, and after a while Dylan closed his as well. The faucet dripped with a slow *plink plink*—he should fix that one of these days—and the rain thudded dully against the window. With the steam in his nose and the moisture sinking into his skin it was a bit like being underwater, very dreamy and peaceful, and for a little while he let his problems recede from the forefront of his mind.

Chris shifted in the water, causing a slight splash, and Dylan opened his eyes. Without really planning to, he reached into the water and brushed his fingers against the characters inscribed on Chris's leg. "What does the tat mean?"

"Wild one."

"Really?"

Chris peeled one eyelid halfway open. "A souvenir of my misspent youth."

"I like it."

Chris snorted softly, but Dylan thought he looked pleased nonetheless. He looked even more pleased when Dylan's wandering hand moved up his leg, briefly stroking the tender skin behind his knee before continuing up the outside of his thigh to his hipbone. The oil had made him feel soft and slightly slick. Dylan wondered what he would taste like.

He had to move onto his knees and scoot forward a little in order to count the ridges of Chris's abs, to draw a line up his sternum, to feel the pebbled flesh of nipples contract under his fingertips. Chris didn't move under his caresses, but his breaths grew a little more shallow, and, as Dylan watched avidly, his cock thickened and filled until the rosy head was bobbing in the silky water.

Chris's upper chest and shoulders were above the water line. Dylan traced a moist trail along them with his index finger, writing words in an imaginary alphabet and drawing arabesques. Next he moved his hand down a bicep that was firm and full, even at rest. His hand dropped into the water again as he petted the inside of Chris's elbow—so delicate—and the lightly haired forearm. When he came to the wrist, Chris flipped his own hand over and laced his fingers with Dylan's, holding on tightly, as if he needed to be saved from drowning. "Feels good," he whispered hoarsely.

Grunting his agreement, Dylan gently pulled his hand away. He wanted to touch Chris's cock—or better yet, to taste it—but instead he set his palm against the hard belly and felt it move as Chris breathed. "You have nice legs," he observed.

"That why you wanted me? 'Cause you saw my legs that first day?"

"No, it was your ass that did the trick for me."

Chris finally peeled open his eyelids, revealing eyes so clear and blue that they reminded Dylan of Crater Lake—unexpected depths, but not cold like those waters. In fact, at the moment they burned with intensity. "What does a guy like you see in someone like me? Just my tight ass?"

Dylan couldn't help but laugh. "I was wondering the same thing. Chris, maybe nobody's ever told you this, but you're goddamn amazing."

"Yeah, I'm real pretty," Chris said with a slight frown.

Dylan pushed the heel of his palm into Chris's stomach. "I wasn't talking about your looks."

There was a long silence during which Chris stared at him so fiercely that Dylan felt as if his skull were being cracked open for a careful examination of his brain. But he couldn't tell what was going through Chris's head, and he was a little afraid. Had he said too much

133

and scared his lover away? But wait—he was supposed to be avoiding getting too entangled, wasn't he?

His formerly peaceful mood was abruptly gone, and he started to stand. But before he could get all the way to his feet, Chris was scrambling out of the tub and launching himself against him with such force that Dylan nearly toppled over. "Tell me," he demanded throatily in Dylan's ear. "Tell me what's so fuckin' amazing about me if it ain't my ass." He was holding Dylan tight, soaking through his clothing.

Dylan realized that he'd been right. Nobody had ever said this to Chris before. "You're brave. You're funny. You're… surprising. In a good way. We haven't really done all that much together—just remodeling and a little shopping and kind of hanging out—but I've been having fun. I feel like I could never get bored with you, not even if I never got in your pants again. You're a hell of a lot smarter than you like to let on. You're generous. You've never judged me." He snuffled deeply at Chris's hair. "You're a good cook, and you always smell goddamn delicious."

For a moment, Dylan really was afraid he'd said too much. But then Chris made a desperate sort of moaning sound and began tugging frantically at Dylan's wet clothes. "You are so gonna get lucky tonight, dude," he growled.

I already have, thought Dylan.

Somehow they ended up on Dylan's bed, Dylan now as bare as Chris, and Dylan's mouth was everywhere on that citrus-scented skin, and Chris was writhing and bucking beneath him. Usually Chris was fairly quiet when they had sex, mostly just uttering a few blasphemies when things got especially intense, but now he was gasping endearments—"Yeah, like that, baby. F-fuck yeah, Dyl. Please. Oh God, p-please."—making sexy little rumbles in his chest, and periodically tugging Dylan's head down by the hair to lick at his jaw line.

The lube was hastily fumbled from the bedside table and cursorily applied to Chris's twitching, welcoming hole. The condom was rolled on with fingers grown clumsy with haste and desire. Chris hooked his feet over Dylan's shoulders, and Dylan held tight to Chris's hips, and it was if Dylan couldn't get in far enough or fast enough to please them, as if they were both striving for some kind of impossible union that was almost within reach. Chris's core was as hot as flames. His head was thrown back, his collarbones prominent, and his neck stretched out. He demanded more and more and Dylan gave it, both of them soaring together with mingled howls and then floating down to land in one another's arms.

Instead of getting dressed and slogging back to his little house, Chris pulled the covers over them both, rolled onto his belly with his arms and legs stretched wide and one arm resting across Dylan's torso, and fell deeply asleep.

Chapter 16

Dylan woke up three times during the night. Part of it was lunar restlessness—the moon would be full the next night—but more than that, he wanted to stare greedily at the man sleeping beside him. There had been only a handful of times in his entire life when he'd actually slept with someone, and he liked it, even though Chris managed to take up two-thirds of the bed and most of the blankets. Dylan wanted to reach over and pet him, to run his fingers through the tousled hair, but he stopped himself because he was afraid that if Chris woke up, maybe he'd go back to his own house.

But when Dylan's eyes fluttered open to the daylight, Chris was still there. His head was propped on one elbow as he stared at his bedmate. "You snore," he announced.

"So do you. And you're a bed hog."

"Your mattress is better than mine."

"Yeah," Dylan agreed, although he'd never actually slept in Chris's bed. "You could use a new one."

Chris reached over and with surprising tenderness pushed the hair out of Dylan's face. He was wearing his half smile, but it didn't reach his eyes, which remained solemn, maybe a little sad. "You ain't never gonna let me in, are you?"

Dylan blinked sleepily at him, not understanding. "You... you want to top next time? 'Cause that's fine with me."

"Ain't what I meant." Chris tapped his finger on the center of Dylan's forehead. "In here."

"I don't… I don't understand."

With a heavy sigh, Chris sat up, dragging the blankets with him and gathering them around his waist. His upper body remained bare, skin golden in the light that escaped the sheets hung as makeshift curtains. "Don't matter," he said.

Dylan was beginning to realize that there were more hazards in spending the night with someone than simply morning breath. He didn't want to talk about feelings, not before his first cup of coffee and probably not after. And not when he could still smell the bath oil on both their bodies, still smell the traces of Chris's come on the bedding. Dylan was half-hard and half-lazy, and what he wanted to do was either fuck or go back to sleep. Instead he sighed and sat up.

"If you're mentioning it, then it does matter."

They were sitting next to each other, backs propped on pillows, both staring at the opposite wall. Dylan hated the wallpaper in here even more than he'd hated the chickens in the kitchen. At least someone could have argued that the chickens had retro kitsch value. This room had malformed brownish flowers. He wondered whether Chris's great uncle had picked out the paper and why he'd chosen that pattern.

"You've always known I'm just a redneck," Chris said quietly. "Kinda guy who pees off his back porch. I didn't even finish high school. Thought for a while about gettin' my GED but never bothered. And after those assholes in the tavern, you know what I… what I used to be. You know about my dumbass family and my ugly shack and… and you know everythin'."

"Yeah, and I told you: I like you just as you are. None of the bad stuff bothers me—well, maybe your taste in music. But really, most of your stuff's all good with me."

"But that ain't the point. You know me, know everything that's important. But you got somethin'… this place you go to in your head… and I can't come in. Some big fucking secret and I can tell it's goddamn important, and you won't tell me what it is."

Dylan hunched his shoulders. He wanted to explain, he really did.

"I can't," he whispered.

"You don't trust me."

Dylan twisted his body to look at Chris, who was staring angrily away, jaw clenched tightly. "No! That's not... goddamn it, that's not it. It's not you, Chris."

Chris's laughter held no humor. "Isn't that what you're supposed to say when you break up with a chick? 'It's not you, it's me'."

Dylan's stomach twisted, and he suddenly felt very cold. "Is that what we're doing? Breaking up?"

"Can't break up if you ain't really together," Chris answered. Finally he turned to face Dylan. He looked sad, pitying maybe, but not angry. "I'm still gonna do this, Dylan. Still gonna work for you and cook for you, and we can still fuck, because I'm willin' to make do with that little. It's more'n I've had before, anyway. And maybe it's for the best, 'cause then you won't break my fuckin' heart when you leave. But—"

"I'm not going to leave!"

"But you deserve more, dude. And you ain't never gonna get more if you keep yourself locked up."

With that pronouncement, Chris pushed off the blankets, stood, and padded to the bathroom.

CHRIS would have stayed and worked with him that day. It's what Dylan had planned, originally. With the kitchen and downstairs bath complete, they could tackle the master bath next. Or maybe they'd get rid of that fucking ugly wallpaper instead.

But Dylan was unsettled by Chris's comments and hated himself for not being able to tell the goddamn truth, making him even more restless than usual this time of month. So he told Chris he needed to work on the Beaverton project, which wasn't a lie, but then he added untruths. "No dinner tonight either. I'm just going to work on through."

Chris's eyes searched Dylan's face, and even though Chris was a grown man—almost two years older than Dylan, in fact—and fully capable of taking care of himself, for a moment he seemed lost and vulnerable. Dylan wanted to gather him in his arms and tell him everything would be all right, but that would be another falsehood.

"If you're done with me, fucking say so," Chris said quietly. "Don't take off like a fucking coward, like—"

Like everyone else has. Dylan knew that's what Chris had intended to say. The poor bastard had abandonment issues, and he'd fallen in with a monster.

Dylan cupped Chris's cheek in one hand. "I'm not done with you, and for the hundredth time, I am not going anywhere."

Relief washed across Chris's features. He nodded once and walked out the back door, letting it slam behind him.

After standing there for several minutes, Dylan walked into the living room, sat down at his drafting table, and booted up his computer. He was likely to end up fired anyway, but he might as well give the project a concerted effort. The minutes ticked by as the blank screen mocked him. He was distracted by the birds zooming and twittering outside his window. After a while he stood and paced the room. Stender might have opined about the inspirational powers of nature, but at the moment Dylan felt as inspired as a chunk of rock.

He stopped in the corner of the room and banged his head against the wall three times. That didn't help either.

Okay then. Maybe Stender was right, or maybe a change of scenery would help. Dylan pulled on his jacket and found his boots where he'd abandoned them the night before. Then he headed across the backyard, glancing at the little barn as he went. Maybe he could design a barn house for his clients, something with soaring ceilings and exposed beams. No. You could find plenty of those in Beaverton already.

The ground was still muddy from the previous night's downpour, so he stepped carefully down the path. Maybe when the blackberries were ripe, he could pick a bunch and bring them to Kay and beg for more pie. Hell, he'd have enough berries for a thousand pies, even after he cleared the brambles from the trail.

Everything was so lush and green down by the pond. He felt that if he stood still too long, he might start sprouting moss himself. It was a time of verdant growth, and he very much looked forward to hunting later that night. The woods would be teeming with new life.

At some point in the distant past a storm had felled a tree near the banks of the pond. Dylan sat on the broad trunk, not caring too much about the damp that seeped through to his butt. The ducks were back, paddling around at the opposite end of the water, this time with a half-dozen fluffy balls in their wake. A part of him thought *prey*, but he smiled as another part, just as adamant, found the ducklings adorable.

If it wasn't going to be a barn house maybe it could be a miniature castle. There would be stone facing throughout—stucco if the clients wanted to save some money—and crenelated towers. He would put in faux arrow slits and a drawbridge over a miniature moat. He'd include a courtyard, of course, maybe with a low fountain for the dogs to splash in, and the interior would have massive timbers and curved archways and a fireplace big enough to roast a pig. Fit for the futon queens. But also clichéd and maybe a bit too Disneyfied for the clients' tastes.

Maybe the key was to think outside the box geographically. He could design a house that would look perfectly at home in, say, Tuscany or Tokyo, in Lima or Lusaka. "A giant yurt," he said out loud, because when you owned thirty acres you could talk to yourself, and there would be nobody around to call you crazy. "A trullo or a yaodong or a mudhif or an izba. A Soviet-era rabbit hutch or a row house without the row." He could put his comparative architecture college course to good use. But no, still too theme-parky, and besides, he doubted any contractor in the Portland area had experience in building structures made of reeds or cow dung.

He could base the house on a historical model. Fake Tudor was overdone, but what about something a little more radical? A Chinook longhouse. An Aleut ulax. A Greek temple or Roman villa. A pyramid. Now the project was starting to sound like something from the Vegas

Strip. "How about a goddamn cave?" he shouted, and the startled ducks quacked at him with disapproval.

His ass was getting cold. He stood and stretched, then scowled at a clump of ferns as if it were to blame for his predicament. He trudged back up the path and—instead of heading straight to the house—he skirted the edge of the bramble, heading for the rows of overgrown Christmas trees. He leaned back against one of them and inhaled deeply. He'd always enjoyed the scent of evergreens, even when his nose had been an ordinary human one.

Although he found this part of the farm slightly unsettling, it drew him nonetheless. It was like a display of entropy in action: the neat, artificial rows of trees gone blurry with seedlings and underbrush and fallen limbs, the trees themselves grown much too tall to fit inside any home. He wondered whether they regretted their missed opportunity to be briefly decorated and worshiped, or whether they reveled in their freedom, like an animal escaping from the slaughterhouse back to the wilderness. Maybe a little of both.

Somehow that line of thought led him to considering Chris, who was also a juxtaposition of domestic and untamed. "Wild one" read the tattoo of the man who used to give blow jobs to straight men in rural tavern men's rooms, who lived without a plan beyond the next few weeks, who lived in a rundown shack and sometimes found it easier to urinate off the back porch than to listen to his toilet gasp and gurgle. But Chris was also a man who knew how to cook, who could build a kitchen or repair an engine, who read Kurt Vonnegut and worried about his lover abandoning him.

Dylan looked up through the broken green canopy, weighed his own heart, and concluded that he liked that mixture, that just-right combination of controlled chaos and undisciplined order: mundane and exotic, safe and risky, domesticated and wild. He didn't have to choose one or another extreme. He could choose balance for his home: overgrown farm and carefully remodeled house. And he could choose it for himself. He could be a good architect, a caring brother, a tender lover, a man who planned for the future and saved for a rainy day. But he could also be a wolf who ran and hunted in the dark forest, a guy who took risks and gave things a shot, even when he knew they probably wouldn't work out.

He was nearly stunned by the force of his epiphany. But even as he stood there, fingers absently stroking the tree's rough bark, an image of a house came into his head. The image was so detailed that it was as if someone had been working on it for weeks, carefully including every feature until a curtain was finally torn away to reveal the finished product. It was a strange house, different from anything he had ever seen.

Dylan whooped with joy and began to run back to the house. It was time to make some plans.

DYLAN could never be certain of the exact moment when the agony of transformation became the elation of power. Tonight he nosed open the back door that he'd earlier left ajar, and he aimed a canine grin at the clear sky. The moon smiled back, seemingly complicit in his joy.

The forest was beckoning him, but first he trotted through the poplar trees. The flickering light of the television was visible through a window, and he could hear sirens and screeching tires from one of the cop shows Chris liked to watch. As a man, Dylan might still feel ambivalent about his relationship with Chris, but a wolf never questions his loyalties. Dylan jogged around the edges of the little house, keeping to the shadows. He sniffed at everything and, when he was satisfied that no threats had been near, pissed at strategic points. Only when he was satisfied that he'd fully announced his presence did he lope back under the trees, heading down the path and around the edge of the pond.

He knew the ducks were there—he could smell them, even many yards away—but he was after different prey tonight. He ran until he was deep in the forest and then paused to sort the diverse scents. The woods were the olfactory equivalent of a complex tapestry, layered and nuanced. He could tell so much more than which creatures had passed this way and when. He also knew their age and gender and state of health, whether they had recently chased or been chased by something else, what they had eaten, and whether they were in season to mate.

One particular odor caught his full attention: blood. He licked his jowls and hurried farther west, down a small gully and then up a steep rise, into a clearing where the smell was very strong. He pricked his ears forward and caught a quiet rustle in a clump of leaves. Creeping carefully, one paw at a time, he inched forward.

He had almost reached his target when saw the animal, frozen in fear. It was a young fawn, much too young to be on its own. It must have become separated from its mother, or perhaps its mother had died. One of the fawn's stick-like legs appeared badly injured. Dylan could have leapt forward and caught it immediately, but he stalked closer instead. It watched him, narrow chest heaving.

The fawn would die soon, of starvation or disease or infection or from falling to a predator. In a way, what Dylan had to offer was the kindest ending possible, and perhaps somehow the small deer sensed that because its breathing slowed, and its soft eyes seemed to almost welcome the wolf.

Dylan pounced. He broke the deer's neck cleanly and quickly, so that the animal only twitched a few times and then died. And then Dylan feasted, filling his belly with the fresh hot meat.

It wasn't a big kill—a lone wolf could manage only so much—but it was a good one, and when he was done licking the blood from his face and paws, Dylan threw back his head and howled in victory.

CHAPTER 17

IT WAS two weeks since the full moon, and Dylan woke alone. Chris usually stayed only every third or fourth night—whether because he was afraid of wearing out his welcome or for other reasons, Dylan didn't know. When his eyes fluttered open he realized he'd been sniffing the air, happily inhaling the delicious scents of frying bacon and percolating coffee. He smiled and gathered a set of clothing before heading downstairs in the buff.

Chris was standing at the stove, his back to Dylan, humming to himself as he fussed with pots and pans.

"Expecting an army for breakfast?" Dylan asked.

Chris turned, and his eyes widened as he saw that Dylan was nude. "Now that's the way to start the mornin'," he said with a leer.

Dylan padded into the room, planted a sloppy kiss on Chris's cheek, and then dodged the groping hand that reached for his ass. "Gotta shower."

"Raincheck, then. We'll save it for when you make your triumphant return."

With a snort, Dylan made his way to the bathroom. He and Chris had begun the master bath remodel just after the full moon, but they were waiting on tile that Dylan had special ordered. In the meantime, Dylan was showering and shaving downstairs. At least the journey wasn't as bad now that the temperatures had warmed a little. But he was really looking forward to completing the master bath—and its shower stall big enough for two.

He didn't dawdle through his morning routine, but he did take special care to shave and trim his soul patch and to make sure he looked presentable in general. From the smile he received from Chris when he emerged, Dylan assumed he'd been successful on that front. "Too bad you're wasting all that hotness on lesbians," Chris said, piling bacon slices on a plate already overflowing with fluffy scrambled eggs. "You pitch a project to a pair of gay guys lookin' like that, and they'll sign up even if you're gonna make 'em live in a doghouse."

Dylan took the plate. "Thanks for the vote of confidence. I think."

They sat opposite one another at the oak table Dylan had bought. Chris ate his bacon with his fingers and then licked off the grease, which was enormously distracting. Dylan opted to use silverware. When the meal was over, Dylan put the dishes in the dishwasher while Chris filled a big insulated cup with coffee and several spoonfuls of sugar. "Break a leg," he said as he handed over the cup.

"I think that's just for acting."

Chris lifted an eyebrow. "So what're you supposed to say for architecture?"

"Um... I think for architecture you're supposed to give the architect a huge kiss."

"Well, I wouldn't wanna break tradition," said Chris. He drew Dylan into his arms and pressed their lips together. Chris tasted good, and for a moment Dylan was sorely tempted to just forget the whole thing, to stay home and have a really good shag. But then Chris was pushing him away and patting his butt proprietarily. "Knock 'em dead, dude."

As he made the long drive into the city, Dylan listened to NPR. He was feeling almost preternaturally calm, maybe because he'd already decided what he was going to do: When the clients shot him down, he was going to resign. He would drive home and fuck Chris through the mattress, and then he'd find another way to get by. He would think of something. He could assist Chris on his intermittent odd jobs. He could raise Christmas trees or free-range organic chickens. He could grow barley and hops and learn to make microbrews. He could learn to bake, charm Kay out of her pie recipe, and make the entire state fat from blackberry pastries. He could open Columbia County's first gay strip club and headline himself and Chris as dancers. He could grow his hair long and wear animal skins and live off deer and the fish from his pond.

He'd fucking figure something out.

The traffic and bustle of the city already seemed a little alien to him. So many people, caught up in their own lives, rushing here and there. As he waited at stoplights he'd look at pedestrians and fellow motorists and wonder what secrets they had. Maybe some of them were werewolves too.

He couldn't help but glance around nervously when he parked in the garage, but there was no sign of Andy. The most sinister thing he saw was a Buick with a Sarah Palin bumper sticker.

Matty smiled worriedly at him as he walked into the office. "It's almost time, Dylan! Quick, let me see the plans."

He clutched the laptop protectively to his chest. "You'll see when everyone else does, Matt." She frowned, and he patted her shoulder. "Nobody's seen yet, okay? Nobody but me. I want to just do the reveal all at once and—" And then run like hell. "—and then see how people react."

She didn't appear especially mollified, but he wasn't going to budge. He hadn't even shown Chris the plans, not even when Chris begged and pleaded and promised the best blow job ever. Dylan waited as she scowled some more, but eventually she shrugged. "Whatever. This better be good."

He was still calm. And he was rather amazed at that.

He was the first one in the conference room, and he just sat there with his laptop closed in front of him. Then Matty came in and shot him a glare before sitting next to him. They didn't speak. She stared at her blue-painted fingernails, and he thought about how nice it felt when Chris nibbled on his earlobes.

Stender and the clients were chatting about an art museum exhibit as they entered the room. Dylan stood and shook hands with

Pomegranate and Cassidy. Stender was smiling serenely, as if he had all the confidence in the world in Dylan. Everyone sat, there was a minute or two of meaningless small talk about traffic and weather, and then everyone was looking expectantly at Dylan.

He smiled and opened his laptop.

"This is something… a little different," he said.

The clients smiled broadly in anticipation. "Perfect!" Cassidy exclaimed. "That's exactly what we're hoping for."

Dylan opened the file and swung the screen around. There was a gasp in three-part harmony—even Stender gasped—and Matty made an irritated click in her throat and scurried around the table so she could see as well. "What's that?" she blurted.

Without losing his cool, Dylan smiled. "Something that probably would've got me kicked out of architecture school." He leaned back in his chair and laced his fingers in his lap. "But I think it's just what's needed here."

It took a few moments, but eventually Stender regained his equilibrium. "Why don't you explain what we're looking at, Dylan?"

"Of course. This is a synthesis. See, I was thinking about suburbs like Beaverton and what they mean. What the street where this house will be built means. And it's sort of a transition, a neither here nor there. I guess at one point it was probably forested and then it was farmland and now it's fairly densely populated by people who mostly work in the city. And even the people themselves—a lot of them are from somewhere else, and after a few years they move on because they have kids and they need a bigger place, or the kids grow up and they want something smaller, or someone gets a job transfer or something. Even when they stay put, people who live in the 'burbs spend their days driving around, going to work, running errands, taking the kids to soccer practice and dentist appointments. Like I said, a place in transition, a place *of* transition."

Everyone was nodding as Dylan spoke. Hopefully that meant they were following him so far, but it didn't mean they'd like the house plans. But he truly didn't care. He felt more confident and more powerful than he ever had—except when he was a wolf. The wolf tracked and hunted. The man designed iconoclastic houses that were commentaries on modern life. Well, one iconoclastic house, anyway.

"This house reflects the influences of history and space and lifestyle on the suburb. I think if you look at some of the individual parts you might recognize them, but I've put them together in a way nobody else has."

Stender leaned forward to squint at the screen. His head was slightly tilted, as if he were trying very hard to understand but hadn't quite grasped it. "I think I see… parts of a mountain lodge," he finally said, not sounding very sure of himself.

Dylan smiled. "Yep. You can see the logs, the chunks of granite. The wood's not real, though—it's formed and stained concrete, just like the Ahwahnee in Yosemite. We could probably do faux granite from concrete too, if you wanted."

"But this sure doesn't look like Yosemite," Cassidy said, pointing at a tower that protruded from the house's west wing.

"That's metal and glass. I've adapted elements from functionalist and neomodern urban buildings there and throughout the house. A little Mies van der Rohe, a little Renzo Piano."

"It sort of reminds me of those skyscrapers you see all over Vancouver," observed Pomegranate.

Dylan grinned at her. "A little of that too."

"I love Vancouver," she replied, smiling back.

"And this wide porch, these little bits of scrollwork you see here and there? I stole those straight from my own farmhouse. I'm not going for a Frankenstein here—I think you can see that different components are interspersed throughout the façade, producing a new and, I hope, harmonious whole."

He waited a few more minutes for everyone to get a good look at the elevation. Then he clicked through a few more exterior drawings, pointing out the rooftop garden with steel walls, the concrete courtyard with the mature fir trees in the middle, the dog run that he'd designed to look like a sort of minimally walled barn, with a green metal roof and a floor of gravel and grass.

"Now let's see the interior," he said. "We have four bedrooms, but these walls can be rolled back to open up the spaces so you can have two or three bigger rooms instead. Same goes with this wall between the kitchen and family room, only it folds instead of rolls. Open it up if you want a big space. Shut it if you don't want guests to see that the kitchen's a mess. The door's made of reclaimed barn wood and stainless steel."

There were many other features to point out: the atrium, the stone fireplaces with recycled glass-tiled mantels, the radiant heating system, the laundry room with terra cotta floor and wire shelving, the closet where a tree trunk—branches and all—was used as a sort of clothes hanger, the bathrooms with cast iron tubs and concrete countertops. Finally, he pulled up the final page, which contained charts of estimated heating and utility costs. "We're going to use a lot of recycled materials, and the whole thing's going to be extremely energy efficient."

There was a long silence. He couldn't tell if his audience was stunned, overwhelmed, or appalled. That was, until Pomegranate suddenly leapt from her chair and ran around the table to throw her arms around him. She barely cleared five feet, which meant she hardly even needed to bend over, and she probably weighed about 90 pounds, but her hug was very strong. She smelled of mint and apples. "It's the most amazing house I've ever seen!" she exclaimed loudly in his ear. "Better than I dreamed of."

She peeled herself away so that Dylan could glance across the table. Cassidy was beaming, Stender looked like a proud parent, and Matty was just staring at him with wide eyes. Dylan took a deep breath and let it out. "Matt and I will have to get together and give you some firmer cost estimates, but—"

"I don't care," interrupted Pomegranate. "We want it, whatever it costs."

Cassidy nodded enthusiastically. "Seriously. If you can pull this off, we can afford it. Pom, I bet we can get Davy and Nix to design some furniture for us." She looked at Dylan. "They usually make the frames for our futons, but I think they've been really itching to try something totally different. Something sort of...."

"Wild?" Dylan finished for her.

"Exactly!"

There were more hugs after that and a double-fisted handshake from Stender, who told Dylan to wait for him in his office while he discussed a few details with the clients. As Dylan stepped out into the hallway, Matty caught his arm. "Who knew you were a frigging genius?" she said.

"Me," he answered with a grin.

She tugged him down the corridor. "So what's the deal? How'd you turn so quickly from pedestrian to inspired?"

He shrugged. "I found my creative wellspring."

"You growing some very special crops out in the boonies, Dyl?"

He pretended to be offended. "You think I need to resort to pharmaceuticals to be creative?"

"No." She stopped and crossed her arms over her chest. "But this wasn't just creative. This was—this was really brilliant, Dyl. I always thought you were too careful to be brilliant. What gives?"

He couldn't give her an honest answer, so he simply shrugged again. And then her eyes went round before her lips curled into a knowing smile. "You found your muse, didn't you?" She punched him lightly in the arm. "Who is he, and how the hell did you find him way out in the middle of nowhere?"

"It's Sasquatch, Matt. I'm having a torrid love affair with Bigfoot."

She actually stuck out her tongue at him, which made him laugh. She socked him again—a little harder this time—and then gave him an awkward one-armed hug. "It's gonna be really fun working out the particulars on this one," she said. "And eventually I'm going to get all the details about Mr. Right."

He hoped his answering smile was enigmatic. He gave her a little wave as they parted and he entered Stender's office. Dylan sat on one of the plastic chairs and stared through the glass top of the desk to the bamboo flooring beneath. He tried to put a name on the emotion he was feeling. Not relieved, because he honestly hadn't been worried about the outcome of today's meeting. He had been fully prepared for rejection, and, although he was pleased to have kept his job, he would have been okay if he hadn't. He supposed he felt a little proud, but the design had come to him so easily that it was almost as if he wasn't the one responsible for it. He understood now why the Greeks had believed in muses, because it was almost as if some benevolent celestial being had handed him the project idea on a platter. Creating the plans had been hard work, but that was mostly just connecting the dots. The shape itself had come into being all at once. He wasn't smug over his success or especially triumphant.

Maybe, he realized, this was simply what happiness felt like when it came without a price or a caveat, without time limits or the threat of dangers ahead.

Stender entered the office about ten minutes later. He sat behind his desk and steepled his hands in front of him and simply smiled, like a monk who was approaching nirvana. "We're going to win awards for this one, Dylan. You're going to make a name for yourself, and other firms will try to hire you away."

That possibility had never occurred to Dylan. "I'll turn them down. I'm satisfied here, as long as I can continue to work from my farm."

"I'm pleased to hear that, and we can safely assume the telecommuting is a success. But if this project goes as well as I hope, there will be a large bonus in it for you." He chuckled. "You can buy more acreage, if you like."

"I'm just glad the clients are happy."

"The clients are ready to adopt you, I think. Expect interest soon from their friends. Do you think you have more of this in you?"

Dylan smiled. "Yeah. I think I do."

CHAPTER 18

TRAFFIC was heavy on the way home, but Dylan barely noticed. In fact, it was probably a minor miracle that he avoided the same death as his parents, in crumpled metal on the highway. But Dylan's head was buzzing with success, with the giddy knowledge that he'd taken a risk and it had come out well. He'd been honest with Stender: he didn't want a different job with a more prestigious firm, and while a bigger salary would be nice, that was only icing on the cake. The main point was that everyone was proud of him, he was proud of himself, and he'd get to keep his new life. His farmhouse was slowly taking shape, like a butterfly emerging from its cocoon. The wolf was satisfied... and then there was Chris.

Dylan refused to acknowledge the remaining dark cloud in his life, however ominous it might be: the secret he still kept from his lover. He could keep that secret a long time, he thought. It was only one day in twenty-eight, anyhow. Besides, Chris would probably get tired of Dylan's personal quirks—including his snoring and his sometimes prissy housekeeping habits—long before he figured out Dylan was a supernatural beast.

He could smell Chris's welcome even before he opened the door—roasting meat that made his stomach rumble demandingly, and potatoes maybe, and several other delicious smells. He crept inside so quietly that Chris didn't hear him—the other man was too busy stirring a pot and singing "Honky Tonk Women" loudly and off-key. Dylan paused in the doorway to watch, thinking that it wasn't the granite or the tile or the expensive appliances that made a kitchen real, but this:

good food being prepared by someone you loved.

Chris must have felt Dylan's gaze because he stopped singing and whirled around, spoon still clutched in his hand. "You kinda creep up on folks, dontcha?"

"Only you."

"How'd it go?"

Dylan came fully inside and shut the door behind him. He set his laptop case on the counter and tried to keep his face neutral. "Is that dinner intended for celebration or consolation?"

"It'll do for either, but I'd rather it was the first."

"What're we having?"

"Roast beef. Haven't made it in years 'cause it's so damned expensive, and I had to drive all the way to Gaston, to this guy I know who butchers his own beef. Real good stuff, none of them hormones or antibiotics or any of that shit. I threw in some potatoes, too, but we also got noodles with this vegetable sauce you're gonna like. I even made a spice cake for dessert. And if you don't fuckin' tell me right now how it went, you ain't gonna get none of it."

Dylan finally allowed himself to smile, which felt really good. "Clients liked it."

"Whoo-hoo!" Chris whooped loud enough to hurt Dylan's ears. He tossed the spoon onto the counter with a clatter and launched himself across the room, landing in Dylan's welcoming embrace. Their lips met and tongues danced. Chris must have been sampling as he cooked because he tasted amazing. His hands clutched at Dylan's shoulders so tightly that Dylan was certain there would be bruises. He didn't understand the physical intensity until they moved apart—still slightly breathless—and Chris whispered, "This mean you're gonna stay?"

Dylan crushed his lover hard against himself. "Told you. I'm not leaving."

The sound Chris made was almost a sob, but when they separated again his blue eyes were dry and very clear, and his half smile was firmly in place. "Fuckin' hallelujah. You gonna let me see the plans now?"

"After dinner."

Chris poked Dylan's belly. "Now. I wanna see what all the goddamn fuss has been about."

So Dylan opened his computer and brought up the files, and Chris listened as Dylan clicked through images. He gave Chris more or less the same explanation he'd given at the office, and Chris nodded slowly the entire time.

When Dylan was finished, Chris looked at him wide-eyed. "Holy shit. You made that?"

"Well, not yet. Right now it's just a lot of schematics, and Matty and I are still going to have to work out some of the details, so—"

"You fuckin' made that. Jesus, Dyl." The tone of his voice was almost worshipful, like when Dylan had given him an especially good blow job. And that thought made Dylan suddenly and achingly hard.

"How long until dinner's ready?" Dylan asked.

Chris must have read the gleam in Dylan's eyes because he grinned. "No way. I ain't gonna ruin forty bucks worth of meat so you can get your rocks off. You go call Kay and Rick and tell 'em you aren't fired, and this—" He squeezed Dylan's cock through his khakis, making Dylan groan. "—can wait."

Dylan did as he was told, although first he went upstairs so he could change. His brother and sister-in-law were happy for him, and even though Dylan still hadn't admitted to them that he had anything going with Chris, Kay giggled and asked whether Chris had congratulated him properly yet.

He tried to protest. "Kay, we're not—"

"Oh, save it. You admit you're crazy about each other or I'm gonna drive out there right now and ask you about it in front of him."

She would too. Even though Kay was sixty miles away and Chris was downstairs and well out of earshot, Dylan blushed. "I think... I kind of think I'm in love," he whispered into the phone.

Kay wasn't really the squealing type, but she made a loud and happy sound. "I knew it! Does he know it?"

"We're not... we haven't been writing poetry and sprinkling rose petals and tripping hand in hand under rainbows, Kay."

"Just because you have Y chromosomes doesn't mean you can't tell each other how you feel, Dylan. Your penises won't fall off if you do."

"We've kind of...." He sighed. "He knows I don't hate his guts."

"You're such a romantic. Just like your brother. Do you know what he bought me for our last anniversary? A knife sharpener."

Dylan snorted out a laugh. "Maybe he thought you were dull?"

"Hah. So have you told him about your little monthly problem yet?"

When Dylan didn't reply, she made an exasperated noise. "Dylan!"

"I can't! I don't want to... don't want to blow it with him."

"And you think keeping a secret like that is a good way to begin a relationship?"

He sat on his bed, still unmade from when he'd awakened to the smell of breakfast. "That's kind of the thing. You can't tell someone you're a werewolf before you hook up, because then he'll take off. But you can't tell him after either, because then he'll be pissed at you for covering it up for so long."

Her voice was gentle when she answered. "I told you. If he really cares about you he'll deal. But the longer you keep quiet the worse it's gonna be."

He frowned at the floor. He knew she was right, of course.

After a few moments of quiet, Kay sighed again. "Sorry, Dyl. I didn't mean to bring you down after such a great day. Why don't you get off the phone and go make out with your boyfriend?"

Dylan had to smile, remembering back to when he'd fetched a DVD from Kay and Rick's bedroom. He'd glanced at the little bookcase near Kay's bedside and noted a healthy assortment of gay romance titles. He should have known back then that he was in deep trouble.

After he ended the call, Dylan wandered back downstairs, where the smells were even better than before and the table was carefully set. "Don't get any ideas," Chris said as he tipped pasta into a bowl. "I ain't gonna put on no frilly aprons or start meetin' you at the door with a cocktail in my hand."

Dylan gave Chris's ass a healthy squeeze. "Too bad. I bet you'd look good in an apron and nothing else." He smirked as he avoided Chris's clumsy swat and then sat down at the table.

Dinner was delicious. Possibly the best meal he'd ever eaten. The meat was nice and rare and practically melted on his tongue, the vegetable pasta tasted like spring, and by the time he finished off a big slice of cake, his stomach was full enough to make him groan. "That meal was a work of art."

Chris ducked his head, hiding his face under a fall of hair and pretending he wasn't beaming with pleasure.

Dylan did the washing up. Chris had told him it could wait, but Dylan hated to leave the kitchen a mess overnight. It took a while to package up the leftovers and to scrub the pots and pans and dishes. Chris watched him work the entire time, drumming his fingers impatiently on the table.

Finally, Dylan toweled his hands dry. "Wanna come over to my place and watch TV?" Chris asked. Dylan's own television was still packed away in a box, mostly because he didn't have any living room furniture yet. Maybe the futon queens would give him a deal on a fold-up couch.

"It's been a long day. I think I'm going to turn in," Dylan said.

"It's nine o'clock, dude."

"Aren't farmers supposed to be early to bed, early to rise?"

"Yeah, but you ain't growin' nothin' but blackberries and weeds."

"And overgrown Christmas trees." Dylan walked across the

kitchen, hauled Chris to his feet and hooked a finger in his belt loop, drawing their hips together. "Come upstairs with me."

Chris nibbled at the scarred piercing on Dylan's earlobe—the earring had fallen out the first time he changed to a wolf, and the hole had closed when he was human again—but then Chris paused. "You think I'm that easy?"

"I think if an architect gets a big kiss to wish him luck, he deserves a hell of a lot more when his presentation blows them away."

After pretending to consider this for a moment, Chris nodded. "Fair enough."

They didn't wait until they got upstairs to begin undressing. They kicked their shoes off as they crossed the kitchen and almost fell down the stairs when they tried to pull one another's T-shirts off. They fumbled with their flies as they stumbled down the hallway. Dylan stumbled and grabbed Chris's arm for support as his jeans got caught around his shins. By the time they got to the bed, Chris was wearing nothing but a pair of white socks and an impressive erection. Dylan still had his boxers on, but Chris tugged at them impatiently.

"Whaddaya want?" Chris asked him.

Dylan looked his lover over from head to toe and couldn't answer. What didn't he want? It was like asking someone to choose only one of the thirty-one flavors. "Not vanilla," he thought, and then realized he'd said it out loud.

That earned him a raised eyebrow. "I been too tame for you?"

Dylan had to laugh at that, and he caught Chris around the waist to bring him close. "Never. What I meant was you are never vanilla."

"What am I then?" More with the eyebrow.

"I think… I think I'm still too full to think in terms of food metaphors. You're goddamn perfect is what you are. My muse."

"So now you want me in a white gown with a harp or somethin'? Leafy thing around my head?"

Dylan kissed his cheek and at the same time settled his palms on

Chris's bare ass. "No, I think I'm pretty satisfied with you just like this, thanks. But you still helped me out with that house, you know."

"How?"

"You... you had confidence in me. And you taught me that maybe doing something... unusual... is a good idea."

Chris hummed his approval, undulating slightly against Dylan and licking at his shoulder. "Ain't never been a muse before."

"Well, you're awfully damn good at it." And Dylan suddenly fell to his knees, hard enough to hurt, grasped Chris's hips in his hands and nuzzled deeply around the root of his cock. "Smell good too."

If Chris was planning to answer, he didn't get a chance: Dylan slid the crown of Chris's cock between his lips and sucked lightly, and Chris just gasped and grabbed Dylan's hair for support. Dylan liked the taste of him as much as the scent, the bit of saltiness that reminded him of blood, the slick feel against his tongue. He liked knowing that Chris's femoral pulse was so near to him—so near he could almost hear it—and when he moved one hand to Chris's thigh he liked the feel of the hairs against taut skin.

Dylan took Chris in just a little more. He slid his hand to the inside of the thigh and brushed his fingers against the skin behind Chris's balls. Chris huffed out a breath and widened his stance a little, easing Dylan's access. Dylan rewarded him by taking him deeper still and stroking the puckered entrance to Chris's body.

Ignoring his own aching erection, Dylan bobbed his head up and down, sometimes pausing to lick the big vein that ran under Chris's cock or to nibble very lightly around the glans, and all the time he was nudging his finger just barely inside Chris, mindful of the fact that they hadn't yet retrieved the lube.

Almost experimentally, like he wasn't sure how Dylan would react, Chris thrust his hips slightly forward and then back. When Dylan didn't object, Chris repeated the motion. His fingers curled tightly in Dylan's hair, and his breaths came loud and ragged.

"Dyl...." Chris said hoarsely. Dylan would have been willing to continue. But Chris jerked backward slightly, his cock sliding out of Dylan's mouth and banging against his chin. "I want more," Chris said. He held a hand out to help Dylan to his feet, and, although Chris was reaching for the nightstand and the bottle of K-Y, Dylan grabbed at him first and stole a kiss. His lover tasted of the cake's cinnamon and sugar and cloves.

Eventually they collapsed onto the bed. Sometimes when they had sex there was an urgency to it, like teenagers fucking in a car, but as eager as they'd been to undress one another, this time they took it slow. Dylan knew by now which parts of Chris he could caress to incite moans and shudders and pleas for more. Not just the obvious parts, either—although those were plenty fun—but also the creases where legs met torso, the inside of elbows and, most satisfyingly to Dylan, the tender nape of Chris's neck. Chris would purr when Dylan carded fingers through long dark hair and whimper when Dylan sucked on broad, calloused fingers.

Dylan had never had the opportunity to learn another person's body like this, to know its specifics more intimately than he knew his own. The knowledge made him feel giddy and powerful and capable all at once.

And at the same time, Chris was studying him. A diligent scholar, Chris knew that Dylan wanted to smell and taste, and he offered himself up freely, like a feast. Chris had figured out that Dylan didn't mind just a little pain with his pleasure—nothing much, just a soft bite here and a gentle twist there—adding layers of sensation like spices in a meal. And Chris knew when to roll the condom over Dylan's desperate cock, when to spread himself wide and plead to be filled.

They rocked together, joined and sweating, and they gasped each other's names when they came.

"Stay here tonight," Dylan mumbled sleepily when they were done. They were still entwined, neither having the energy to clean up. And then he remembered what Kay had said to him earlier that evening. He couldn't tell Chris about the wolf, he just couldn't. But at least he could open up about the only other secret he held.

"I love you," he whispered, half hoping Chris was already asleep.

But Chris's breathing hitched, and his muscles went tense. Dylan could see his face even in the darkness; Chris's eyes were wide with shock. Without turning his head to look at Dylan, Chris said, "You don't have to say that. I ain't... you can have me anyway. You don't gotta pretend—"

"Not pretending."

Then Chris did turn, and he made one of those sounds that wasn't quite a sob before grabbing Dylan's hair in his fists and drawing their foreheads together. "Fuckin' hell," he rasped, and Dylan smiled.

CHAPTER 19

CHRIS spent four nights in a row in Dylan's bed. Since Chris usually fell asleep first, Dylan liked to lie there in the dark and listen to him breathe, to burrow his nose into the crook of the sleeping man's neck and inhale the scents of sweat and food and shampoo and soap and sex and himself. Especially himself—it gave him a strange thrill to know that Chris smelled of him, as if it were a sign of belonging that everyone would recognize. Nobody would, of course, at least nobody entirely human, but Dylan knew, and that was enough.

Four nights in a row, Dylan fell asleep feeling the rise and fall of Chris's chest beside him. And Dylan would wake up two or three times—he'd always been a light sleeper—and notice the way Chris was touching him in his sleep. A hand thrown casually on top of Dylan's stomach, a naked thigh pressed against his, a foot hooked over one of Dylan's legs. Chris was a heavy sleeper, and Dylan learned that he could brush the dark hair away from Chris's face and trace a finger over full, slightly slack lips, and Chris would barely twitch. Dylan liked that as well. It made him feel protective, which was strange, because what was there to protect Chris from in his own home? Except Dylan himself, of course, but that didn't bear thinking of.

And four mornings in a row Chris awakened first and slithered under the blankets so that Dylan was aroused—in both senses of the word—by a tongue on his cock or by a mouth gently sucking on his balls. He was pretty sure that was the best possible way to begin the morning.

Even better, while Dylan still lazed in bed, cozy under the

blankets and groggy in his postcoital doze, Chris went downstairs and made eggs or french toast or pancakes. He didn't go so far as to bring it to Dylan in bed on a tray—instead he bellowed from downstairs when it was ready—but it was still heavenly for Dylan to slip on a pair of sweats and a tee and pad down to the kitchen and discover hot food and coffee and a hotter boyfriend waiting for him.

After eating, the two of them would work on Dylan's house for a while, giving him hope that the place would someday be fully habitable. Maybe he'd invite Rick and Kay over for dinner, if Chris was willing to cook for them. Maybe Matty could come over too. She kept hinting about wanting to see the place. Dylan had abandoned his few other friends after he became a werewolf, but even though his current circle remained small, he was pleased with its caliber. Chris never mentioned friends of his own, and Dylan hadn't wanted to push, but maybe soon there would be a good opportunity to ask a few gentle questions.

Dylan made them lunch every day. He could manage sandwiches and chips, at least.

In the afternoons, Chris went back to his own place. Sometimes he tinkered with his cars and returned later, smelling like oil and metal. Sometimes he read or watched TV. In the meantime, Dylan would Skype Matty, and they'd e-mail files back and forth, tinkering with the Beaverton plans. Chris would start dinner while Dylan was still working, and soon wonderful smells would start distracting him. Dylan and Matty would sign off, the meal would be served, and then there was TV and sex, or sex and TV, or sometimes both at the same time. Cuddling tended to follow, although Dylan didn't quite admit that part to himself, and probably neither did Chris.

It was all much more domestic than Dylan had ever imagined, and he was happy. But when he woke up on the fourth morning, his skin was itching strangely, and he remembered with a start that the moon would be full that night.

He tried to go about the day as normally as possible, but Chris kept frowning at him as if he were trying to figure out what was wrong. Finally, as they struggled to install a cabinet, Chris went one way and

Dylan went the other and the result was a sharp impact of wood on Dylan's foot. "Goddamn it!" he snapped.

"What the hell's wrong with you?" Chris demanded.

"You just dropped a hundred fucking pounds on me, that's what's wrong."

"Didn't drop it by myself, dude, and you're wearin' boots. Pull up your panties and deal."

Dylan just growled at him and stomped out of the room. He wanted to throw things or punch things or just fucking bite. Instead he stood at his window, glaring at a jay that was scolding noisily from a nearby fir branch.

Maybe five minutes later, muted footsteps approached. Chris didn't say anything, and Dylan didn't turn around. Eventually, Dylan allowed his stiff shoulders to slump a little. "Sorry," he muttered.

"Am I doin' somethin' to piss you off? 'Cause if so you better tell me—I ain't gonna figure it out on my own. No fancy college degree, remember?"

Dylan turned around to find that little smile curling at the corner of Chris's lips, but there was a softness in his eyes that reminded Dylan a little of the fawn he'd killed the previous month. He sighed and settled one hand on Chris's broad shoulder. "You're not doing anything wrong. I just...." He closed his eyes for a moment and then opened them. "Maybe I need a little space."

He felt Chris's muscles tense. "Yeah. Okay. Be seein' you." Chris began to walk away, but Dylan caught his arm.

"Don't. Fuck, this is hard. I haven't done this before, okay? It's always just been me, and when I've... been in a pissy mood... nobody else had to suffer. Let me have some time to myself. Please. I'll be better by tomorrow, I promise."

Chris gave him a long and skeptical look but didn't try to disentangle himself. Dylan pulled him close and kissed the tender skin just under his ear. "Go home, Chris. I'll hunt up dinner myself for a change. You can watch that stupid lawyer show tonight—the one I hate—and eat all the garlic beef jerky you want. Tomorrow… tomorrow I'll make up for it. There's this great steak place in the city, over on Burnside. I'll see if I can get us a reservation."

Chris pulled slightly away. "If you're gonna kick me to the curb just tell me straight, man. Don't wanna play any fuckin' games."

"God, Chris, I told you. I love you. I've never said that to anyone. I'm not kicking you anywhere. Just give me tonight. Please."

With a slight shudder, Chris gave a single nod. He allowed his head to rest against Dylan's for just a moment, and then he gently disengaged his arm. "I'm gonna go drink a bunch of that cheap beer you think you're too good for."

Dylan gave him a small smile. "Okay. I'll switch you back to the good stuff tomorrow."

He watched Chris walk away.

He intended to work on the plans that afternoon, but he simply couldn't settle. He paced the house, absently cataloging future projects in his head. He seemed to find himself in the yellow bedroom often, looking through the window toward Chris's property. The poplars had fully leafed out, so now he could catch only a slight, teasing glimpse of Chris's back porch through the gap in the trees. Although out of his line of sight, he knew the stacks of bottles and cans were still there.

Fifteen minutes before sunset, he stripped off his clothing and left it folded neatly on the bed. Shivering slightly, he made his way downstairs and opened the back door a few inches. Since the wolf couldn't manage the doorknob, he'd probably just bash the door down if it weren't slightly ajar. "Should install a goddamn dog door," he said aloud.

Then he waited, bouncing nervously on the balls of his feet, preparing for the pain to begin. He'd spent all afternoon pretending he wasn't thinking about Chris and how he might finally break the news to him. He could picture himself handing Chris a collar and asking, "How do you feel about pets? Do you have any dander allergies?" Yeah, that would go well. As for the continuing worry about the wolf harming Chris—well, he was going to have to deal with that later too. For tonight at least, he hoped Chris was safely indoors, garlic-breathed and slightly buzzed, watching unnaturally attractive attorneys spend more time fucking and scheming than practicing law.

When the pain hit, Dylan dropped to the floor. He had a moment to think that maybe next time he should transmogrify in a room that was carpeted, and then he couldn't think of anything at all except the agony.

But oh, it was worth it. It always was.

Four-legged, he bounded joyfully out of the house and into the night. His survey of Chris's house took only a few minutes. When he was satisfied that he'd marked his territory assertively enough, he ran back under the poplars, down the path, around the pond.

He found deer again tonight—the woods were full of them—but these were strong and healthy, and he regretfully decided they were too much for him. He felt a brief sadness that he didn't have a companion to hunt with, but wolves don't dwell long on what might be, so soon enough he was trotting with his nose to the ground, chasing another intriguing scent.

Like last time, he killed a rabbit—this one fat with late spring greenery—then a small rodent of some kind. It was too tiny to be more than a nibble to him, but it was fun to chase, and it crunched satisfyingly between his jaws. After that he was no longer hungry, and his urge to kill was gone, so he spent a long and happy time simply running through the forest, reading it the way a man might read the newspaper. It was a joy to leap and clamber so effortlessly, to put on short bursts of speed that made the tree trunks seem to fly by. He sniffed and dug and ran and pissed, and when he found something long dead and delightfully stinky he fell down on his back and rolled in it.

About two hours before sunrise he picked up speed again and circled back to his own farm. He was already within smelling distance of his pond when he heard the howl.

It wasn't the yip of a coyote or the miserable wail of a dog left outside. This was a wolf, and it was calling a challenge. There was no question in Dylan's mind at whom that challenge was aimed.

Black rage filled his heart, but so did fear. He ran faster, growling almost inaudibly as he went. His hackles were up, and his lips had curled back from his long teeth. He crashed through the ferns at the edge of the pond, startling the ducks out of their sleeping place with squawks of alarm, but he paid them no mind. He tore up the path, and the howl came again, nearer. Much nearer, in fact—the sound originated just beyond the poplars.

Dylan had read up on wolves—after the shock of what he'd become had abated slightly. He wasn't sure if everything he'd learned about *Canis lupus* applied to him as well, but if wolves could reach a top speed of over thirty-five miles per hour, he was certain he was going at least that fast right now. His paws barely touched the ground as he surged to the top of the slope, raced across his mossy and debris-littered backyard, and zoomed through the line of trees.

As he burst out of the poplars, he saw that the back door to Chris's house was wide open, spilling light onto the planks and cinderblocks and the colorful towers of glass and aluminum. At the same time, the smell hit him—a wolf. And the scent was familiar.

The howl came for a third time, its proximity almost hurting his sensitive ears. It was followed by a thud and a cry. A human cry. Also familiar.

Dylan cleared the back porch in one long leap and landed just inside the little house. A dark wolf—sooty black in contrast to Dylan's tawny gray-brown—stood ten feet away. Its head was lowered threateningly, and its teeth were bared. Yellow eyes gleamed in the light from the cheap overhead fixture. Tail held stiffly straight, he answered Dylan's growl. The two sounds rumbled against the crappy wood paneling and seemed to make the entire house vibrate. The dark wolf was slightly shorter than Dylan but more solidly built, and Dylan knew exactly how capable that animal was of tearing flesh as if it were paper. He'd once felt those sharp teeth himself.

"Oh fuck!" Chris was sprawled on the floor just behind Dylan's alpha, trapped in a corner by the big wolf. Dylan couldn't scent blood, so Chris was probably uninjured, but the acrid reek of fear was pouring from him. The odor filled the room and made Dylan feel slightly dizzy.

The human smelled like prey, and Dylan wanted to kill.

Dylan took a stiff and cautious step forward, and then so did Andy. Chris took the opportunity to scramble to his feet, but Andy immediately spun and snapped at him, fangs missing Chris's belly by mere inches. "Fuck!" Chris yelled again and backed up until he was pressed tightly against the wall. He put his hands out protectively, as if that would do any good, and his wide eyes darted desperately around the room. "Nice doggies," he said hoarsely. "Nice fuckin' goddamn wolves." His voice broke a little on the last word.

Apparently satisfied with the human's submission, Andy ignored him. Instead he raised his head and tail and, continuing a warning growl, locked eyes with Dylan. The message was clear: submit to your alpha.

And for a moment, Dylan was torn. The wolf belonged to Andy, but the man belonged to Chris. A wolf doesn't question his loyalties, but what does he do when those loyalties conflict? He wanted his pack, and he wanted his lover. He was torn between a run through the trees and a passionate tumble in his bed. And even in his canine form he sensed he couldn't have both. He wouldn't do to Chris what Andy had done to Dylan, and in any case, he wouldn't be willing to share Chris with Andy. But... Andy was his alpha, and Dylan knew his alpha would never turn him away for being a monster.

As Dylan vacillated, Andy relaxed just a bit. Chris tried to dart past him, probably heading for the kitchen and his phone, but Andy reacted, bashing the side of his squarish head heavily into Chris's gut. Chris *oofed* and fell, and Andy was instantly on top of him, paws on his shoulders, teeth inches from Chris's vulnerable throat. But he didn't bite—not yet. Instead, he turned his head to look at Dylan. With a feral grin, he invited his beta to join in the kill.

And at that instant, Dylan's uncertainty was gone.

He didn't even bother to growl. He simply leaped, and his momentum bore Andy off Chris and onto the carpet. But Andy managed to keep his feet and suffered only a small graze from Dylan's teeth. He was immediately on the attack, going straight for Dylan's throat.

Dylan screamed when the fangs cut into his skin, but his cry was more from anger than pain. Whatever human thoughts had been bouncing around in his skull evaporated. For the moment he was strictly animal, and he *knew* this dance in a way no man had known it for thousands of years. Conquer or be defeated, master or be mastered, kill or die.

Oh, he wanted to kill.

Snarls and roars reverberated throughout the small room as the wolves' powerful bodies crashed into one another. The coffee table splintered, and the sofa overturned. Something glass shattered and was followed by the thud of falling books. Dylan quickly lost track of what Chris was doing. He focused only on what was important—protecting himself while trying to rip out the other wolf's throat.

Teeth and claws tore into Dylan's flanks. Andy had a weight advantage. He managed to knock Dylan onto his side, then shredded a great bloody gouge from his belly. But Dylan was on his feet again before Andy could deliver a lethal blow. Dylan was favoring one hind leg, but he continued to move quickly, and he was still a few inches taller than Andy. He sank his teeth into the base of Andy's neck. It wasn't a killing bite—too much skin and fur to get at the spine—but it rendered Andy unable to swing around and bite back.

Dylan bit harder. The blood flooding his mouth tasted wonderful—hot and fresh and thrumming with life—and the sensation of fangs sinking to their roots was lovely. Hunting was good, but this was better, an adversary fighting back. Never before had Dylan had the opportunity to use his power to the full, to strain every fiber of muscle and tendon and bone into what he was doing.

Andy's front legs collapsed, and Dylan fell on top of him. But when Dylan opened his jaws to reposition them closer to an artery or an airway, Andy bucked and swiped with one huge paw. Thick claws tore across the right side of Dylan's face. He was immediately blinded on that side, whether from blood or actual damage to the eye he couldn't tell, and it felt like the flesh was hanging from his muzzle in flaps.

Andy took advantage of Dylan's pain, pushing his way upright and lunging at Dylan's neck.

Teeth crashed against teeth, skin was flayed. Droplets of blood flew through the air and splattered against Dylan's ears and back. Andy's jaws began to close at Dylan's throat, and he felt the despair of approaching death.

Chris, he thought, a spark of humanity reviving. *Save Chris.*

He twisted and heaved and didn't care when more of his body was slashed as he managed to knock Andy's grip free. Before Andy could recover, Dylan was on him. His mouth closed over the black wolf's throat, and Dylan bit and ground with all his might.

Andy made a frantic howling noise, but it ended with a shriek and then a choking gargle. More blood filled Dylan's mouth. His muzzle was bathed in it, his left eye as blinded as his right. He could smell nothing else, taste nothing else, and he felt the very moment that Andy's heart faltered and then stopped.

Only when the black wolf lay motionless beneath him did Dylan unlock his aching jaws. He was positioned atop Andy during the death throes, and now he struggled to regain his footing. As he did, the furry body beneath him wavered and shifted, becoming the battered corpse of a naked man. Dylan blinked and swung his head around, searching.

Chris was there, still near the kitchen doorway. His mouth and eyes were wide with shock, but he'd managed to grab a leg from the broken coffee table. He held it firmly in two hands, as if it were a baseball bat, and stared at Dylan. "What the *fuck?*" he whispered.

Dylan discovered that he had a sense of humor, even as a wolf. Or maybe sunrise was very near. In any case, there was something funny about the way Chris stood there, holding his ground against wolves with only a piece of furniture as a weapon. Dylan huffed out an amused bark, took a wobbling step toward the back door, and collapsed into darkness.

CHAPTER 20

THE light fixture overhead was a cheap plastic one, square and slightly yellowed with age. One of the three bulbs was burned out, but he could still see the silhouettes of insect corpses. A dusty cobweb led from one corner of the fixture to the textured ceiling. It all looked vaguely familiar, but his head was too muzzy to figure out why.

He couldn't recall where he was or how he'd gotten there. He moved just a little, and the searing pain almost made him black out. And then he remembered.

"Chris?" he tried to say, but it came out an incoherent croak.

"Goddamn it! Stay still!" A big hand pinned his shoulder down. Dylan would have fought, but the scent finally registered, and he stilled at once.

With some difficulty—and more pain—he rolled his head slightly to the side. "Chris," he said again, this time in a hoarse whisper.

Chris's usually tan face was pale as paper, and Dylan could see the whites of his eyes all the way around his irises. "You gonna die?"

Dylan had to think about that. He was in worse pain than he'd ever experienced before, so much that it took him some time to localize the sources of his agony. The right side of his face hurt and so did his left leg, but his belly was the worst. It felt as if something had taken a large bite from his midsection—which, of course, something had. But his consciousness felt fully tacked on, and he figured if he wasn't fading away he was probably not mortally wounded. "No," he answered, with slightly more confidence than he felt.

Chris licked his lips nervously. "I... I ain't called for an ambulance. I didn't think.... You want me to?"

Dylan pictured trying to explain his injuries to doctors and what would happen to him if medical professionals discovered he wasn't exactly... normal. "No. Please don't."

"Dyl—Dylan. You're hurt really bad. I don't.... Fuck. I don't know what to do." There was a raw edge to his voice, and Dylan didn't know whether he was hearing near panic or the onset of shock. Either would be justified under the circumstances.

He thought about the small scratches and scrapes he'd received during each monthly foray into the woods and the way they had faded to nothing by the following evening. He'd received a lot more than scratches from Andy tonight, but maybe these wounds would heal on their own as well. It was strange how little he knew about his own capabilities and limitations. Was the old myth about silver bullets true, and if so, did that mean he couldn't be killed by more usual methods? But no—he'd killed Andy with his teeth, hadn't he?

"Dylan?" Chris's concern seemed to have grown as Dylan remained lost in thought. "Are you—"

"Andy. Where's Andy?" Now Dylan felt close to panic as well. What if Andy was only wounded and was lurking somewhere nearby, waiting to attack Chris?

Chris shook his head. "In the other room."

"Dead?"

"Just about fuckin' decapitated."

Dylan let out a long sigh of relief, which hurt. He was in Chris's bed, he realized, probably ruining the bedding with his blood. "You have bandages?" he asked.

"I got... I got fuckin' Band-Aids. Not... not what you need." Chris chewed on his lower lip and eyed Dylan's torso. "I gotta take you to the hospital, dude."

"No!" Dylan said it so forcefully that he grunted in pain. More quietly, but with a shaky voice, he added, "Please. Please don't. I'll be okay. Just... just gotta rest."

Chris reached for him but then drew his hand back without quite touching. "I can't... can't...." The expression on his face was almost as painful as Dylan's wounds.

And then a terrible thought made its way through Dylan's thick head. "Did you get bitten?"

Chris shook his head mutely, and Dylan sighed again. Chris just stared at him. "I'm sorry," Dylan said, so quietly he wasn't sure whether Chris could hear. He wanted to say more, although he wasn't sure quite what, but suddenly his tongue felt thick, and his eyes were impossibly heavy. He didn't want to leave Chris with this mess to clean up. "Call Rick," he rasped before the gray overtook him.

WHEN he woke again there were new voices. At first he couldn't draw any meaning from them—they were like the talking adults in the old Peanuts cartoons. But like a radio station coming into range, the voices gradually became more distinct, and he recognized them: Rick's was a deep rumble, while Kay's was higher-pitched and tight with tension.

The pain had receded a little, but there was a strange rigidity around his body that he realized must be bandages. He felt so weak that even blinking took enormous effort. It took several seconds before he collected enough energy to say, "Hey?"

Immediately, all conversation stopped and frowning faces appeared over him. "Don't move!" Kay commanded firmly.

"Okay." There wasn't much risk of that anyway. "Is Chris... is he all right?"

Kay and Rick exchanged a glance that he couldn't read, and then Rick nodded. "He isn't hurt, if that's what you mean."

"Where...?"

"He's... out." Rick squeezed his eyes closed and then opened them, and for just a moment he looked so much like their father that Dylan almost cried out. "He's, um, burying... the body. We figured getting the police involved was probably a bad idea, and Chris says he can, uh, hide it somewhere on your property. Is anyone going to be looking for that guy?"

Dylan considered the question. He didn't really know anything about Andy—whether he had any family or friends, if he had a job of some kind. He didn't even know how he had become a werewolf or what had become of Andy's alpha. But deep in his injured gut, Dylan was pretty sure Andy had been alone in the world. "No," he answered. "He probably has a motorcycle somewhere nearby, though."

Rick nodded. "Okay. We'll look for it."

Kay pushed a curl out of Dylan's face. "Sweetie, what can we do to help?"

"You already did," Dylan said, waving his hand a little, trying to indicate his somewhat mummified state. "Thanks."

"You're healing really fast," said Rick. "We could practically watch you get better while we were patching you up. I guess that's a werewolf thing."

"I guess," Dylan agreed. And he supposed he should have asked a lot of questions, but suddenly, all he could remember was the expression of horror on Chris's face right after Dylan killed Andy. Maybe surviving the fight wasn't the best outcome after all. "Can I have some water?" he asked quietly.

Kay nodded, left the room, and returned a moment later with a glass. Rick helped Dylan prop up his head so he could swallow a few sips. It was tepid and slightly metallic, and it tasted wonderful. But even that much effort was enough to wear him out, and his head fell back onto Chris's pillow.

"Rest," Kay said kindly. "Everything's fine for now."

"But... Chris...."

Another look was exchanged over his head, and Rick grimaced unhappily. "I don't think it's a good idea to move you yet. Chris said you can stay here." *For now*, was the unstated addendum.

Kay brushed more hair from Dylan's face, and Rick squeezed his shoulder. Dylan closed his eyes and waited for the welcome abyss of sleep.

NOISES woke him again: shuffled footsteps, the monstrous-sounding flush of Chris's toilet, water running for a few seconds.

Dylan discovered that he could move a little, although he was very stiff and sore. He managed to prop himself slightly upright on the pillow so he had a better view when Chris entered the room. Chris's steps faltered slightly when he saw that Dylan was up. "You ain't dead," he said gruffly and tossed some clothing into the corner of the room.

"I don't think so." Dylan saw that a half glass of water had been left at the bedside. He moved his arm cautiously and grasped the glass, but when his hand shook and he seemed in danger of dropping it, Chris darted over and grabbed his wrist to steady him. He helped guide the cup to Dylan's mouth so he could drink. "Thank you," Dylan said softly when the water was gone.

Chris set the empty glass back on the table. "You wanna eat?"

Usually Dylan was ravenous after he had changed, but right now he wasn't sure he could keep anything down. "Not now."

Chris hovered uncertainly, his face set in a scowl. When he turned in the direction of the door, Dylan was suddenly terrified to be left alone. He reached up and grabbed Chris's arm. Chris looked down at his hand and then gently pulled away.

"Rick and Kay?" Dylan asked miserably.

"Sent 'em home. Don't need 'em now."

"Will you...." Dylan cleared his throat. "What happened?"

Chris looked away, narrowing his eyes at a frayed Allman Brothers poster on the wall. His hands hung at his sides, clenching and unclenching rhythmically. "Stayed up late and fell asleep on the couch, then I woke up a while later. Couch hurts my fuckin' back. I was just about to go to bed when I heard this noise out back. Shit gettin' knocked over. I thought it was a stray cat or somethin', and I opened the back door to scare it away. But I saw a big fuckin' dog, and it came after me. I got inside and slammed the door, and that bastard just crashed on through."

"The door wasn't reinforced," Dylan muttered, earning himself a frown.

"It's just a goddamn door. Never needed no reinforcing before. The dog got me in a corner, just pinned me there, and that's when I saw it wasn't no dog. I thought maybe some asshole had one of them wolf-hybrid pets. You know, the ones they claim are half malamute or somethin' so they can keep 'em. And that goddamn wolf kept me trapped there and howled."

"I heard him."

Chris's shoulders slumped a little, and his gravelly voice grew very quiet. "When you—when the other wolf came in, I thought I was gonna die. Thought maybe there was a whole fuckin' pack out there. Stupid goddamn way to die, too—torn apart by wolves in my own living room."

Dylan nodded. He'd once almost faced the same fate himself.

With a slight shudder, Chris went on. "And then you—well, I guess you know the rest. You turned on him. Fought him."

"He was going to hurt you."

Chris paused for a moment, his frown deepening. "I didn't understand what the fuck was goin' on, and then he... he *changed*. He fuckin' morphed like somethin' in a bad movie and then... then he was just a dead guy, and you...." He shook his head. "I looked in that wolf's eyes, and I saw you lookin' back. You kinda collapsed. I was still tryin' to figure out what the fuck to do when you changed too. I thought you were dead at first!" he added accusingly.

"I'm sorry," said Dylan, because what else was there to say?

Chris walked across the small bedroom and stood facing his dresser, his back to Dylan. "I wasn't sure what to do."

"It's not like most people have contingency plans for that scenario, Chris. You did fine."

Chris was silent for a very long time. At first, Dylan wished he could see his face, but then he reconsidered. He didn't want to see what was there. Disgust? Hatred? Fear? Rage? "I'm sorry," he whispered again, helplessly.

Suddenly Chris whirled around. "What the *fuck*, Dylan? What the everlastin' fuck?"

"I… it happened a couple years ago. Andy did it."

"So you go all *Call of the Wild* when the moon is full, just like in a horror flick?"

"Yeah."

"Can you control it?"

Dylan shook his head slightly. "No. Can't stop it. Once a month I have to be a wolf. And… I'm a real wolf then, Chris. I hunt."

"People?" Chris asked in a tight voice.

"The first time, when I didn't know what was going to happen, Andy showed up again and we chased… we caught a man. Andy killed him. I ran. After that I tried locking myself up, but… but that wasn't working too well."

"That's why you moved to the sticks."

"I've been hunting animals in the forest. No people, but I have to hunt, Chris. I have to."

Chris's eyes were as flat and reflective as a frozen lake. "A fuckin' werewolf." His voice was flat too.

"Yeah," Dylan sighed.

"I been livin' next to a werewolf, and I been workin' with him, cookin' for him. Been fuckin' him."

"Yeah."

There went the fists again. Open, closed. Open, closed. "You can stay here 'til you're on your feet again. Then get out of my goddamn life."

Dylan had known those words were coming—hell, he'd been expecting them for months. But even though he had braced himself for them, they still ripped into him, causing pain worse than anything Andy

176

had done. It increased his distress to know these emotional wounds wouldn't heal anywhere near as fast as the physical ones.

"Chris, I—" He stopped, unsure of what to say. Not *I'm sorry* again—those words felt so meaningless. Not *Please don't make me go,* because begging wouldn't help. Not *I love you*, because that was surely the last thing Chris wanted to hear. Dylan swallowed thickly. The taste of Andy's blood was still on his tongue. "I'm glad you weren't bitten," he finally said.

Chris worked his jaw and shot him a look of pure fury before stomping out of the room.

CHAPTER 21

IT WOULD have been easier if Chris didn't touch him. But Chris did touch him. He held Dylan's hand steady until Dylan could eat and drink on his own. He more or less dragged Dylan to the bathroom and, humiliatingly, helped him on and off the toilet. He unwrapped miles of bandages, and they both looked down in amazement at the long pink scars across Dylan's torso—scars that had been open wounds only two days earlier. Chris's touches were never harsh—they were patient and firm and purely clinical. They were torture.

Chris continued to cook for Dylan, bringing him soup and crackers and later a thick, meaty stew with hunks of bread on the side. He brought water and OJ and coffee. And when Dylan could sit upright for extended periods of time, Chris tossed a couple of paperbacks onto the mattress beside him.

But Chris barely spoke, other than a few monosyllabic efforts to find out when Dylan had to piss and whether he was hungry again. And even though the couch hurt Chris's back, that's where he slept every night. One room over, a world away.

Five days after the full moon, Dylan wrapped a blanket around himself like a toga and—as Chris watched impassively from the kitchen doorway—made a few hesitant circuits of the rooms, trying not to notice the bloodstains on the living room carpet. When Dylan didn't fall, he decided he was well enough to manage on his own. He hovered at the back door, which had not yet been repaired. "Um, I'll return your blanket later," he said.

"Don't bother."

Of course. Chris didn't want to see Dylan again or have anything to do with him, even if it meant losing bedding. Fine, Dylan decided. He could leave the blanket on Chris's front porch sometime, along with the considerable amount of cash he was owed for his renovation work and some extra to cover the damage to his house.

It was sunny and warm outside, and the glare made Dylan squint. He looked over at the poplars. He could just make out his own rooftop and small bits of his siding behind the trees. Then he turned and faced Chris, who hadn't moved from his spot near the kitchen. "Chris, I...." Dylan swallowed. He'd almost apologized again. "Thank you. For... for taking care of me. I know you didn't—well, thank you. You saved my life."

"Owed you that," Chris said with a slight growl.

Dylan didn't see it that way. Yes, he might have stopped Andy from harming Chris, but if it weren't for Dylan, Chris never would have been in danger to begin with. He wasn't about to argue, though. Instead he simply stood there, wanting to say something but unable to find the words. Finally, he gave a single jerky nod and limped across the porch.

Andy must have been inside Dylan's house before he went over to Chris's. The place reeked of canine urine, and there were piss stains on the walls and rugs. The smell made Dylan's stomach lurch so badly that he stumbled to the bathroom and puked up the toast and eggs Chris had given him for breakfast.

Afterward, he glanced in the mirror. His soul patch had morphed into a true beard, and he was sporting a mustache as well. He'd just shave everything off later. The wound to his face had left a scar, but it was close to the hairline and therefore invisible unless he swept his hair back. He was almost disappointed by that—he felt he should have a more obvious mark of his own failure to adequately protect Chris, some way to be recognized, in the way they used to brand criminals.

He wandered through his empty rooms, wiping his mouth with the back of his hand. He wasn't yet in good enough shape to clean, and he was going to have to find someone to help him finish the remodeling. At the moment, his only operational bathroom was downstairs. "Shit," he said out loud. He was too exhausted to deal with any of it just then. He made his way very slowly upstairs, clutching the banister for support, and shuffled down the long hallway. His bed was exactly as he'd left it, clothing still folded neatly near the footboard. He let the borrowed blanket drop from his shoulders and then climbed tiredly between sheets that still smelled of Chris.

"YOU sure you're going to be able to cook for yourself, kid?" Rick asked doubtfully as he shut the fridge.

"As well as I ever have. I'm feeling pretty good now, anyway. Just kind of sore."

"That guy just about gutted you."

"Yeah, but now all my insides are firmly inside again."

Rick crossed the room and sat at the table across from him. "Kay sent one of her pies, you know. Wouldn't even let me have a piece."

"I saw. Thanks. Thanks for everything."

"'S what family's for." Rick reached for the salt and pepper shakers and started toying with them, rolling them a little between his palms and pushing them gently back and forth across the polished wood. He didn't look at Dylan. "How are you doing?"

"Told you. I'm still looking a little Frankensteinish, but I'm okay. I've been having to do a lot of catch-up on the Beaverton project. The clients are really chomping at the bit to break ground. But it's going more smoothly than I expected and—"

"That's not what I meant." Rick lifted his head and pinned Dylan with his sharp gaze.

Dylan sighed. "Did Kay put you up to this?"

"She might've hinted. But you know, I care too, Dyldo."

"I'm not some kind of brokenhearted Victorian maiden, Dickhead. I'm not going to lock myself in the attic and write poems until I overdose on laudanum."

"You've had a tough time of it lately."

"My own damn fault," Dylan replied.

"Part of it, yeah. But have you noticed that it isn't as bad as it could've been?"

"I murdered someone and lost the man I lo—someone I cared about."

"You *saved* the guy you care about, asshole." Rick shoved the shakers away impatiently. "You were so worried for so long that you might attack Chris, but when push came to shove you put your life on the line to rescue him. You're not a monster, Dyl, not even when you're a wolf. You wouldn't hurt the people you love."

In his grief, that thought hadn't occurred to Dylan, but Rick was right. Even as a wolf he had recognized that Chris was his, a member of his pack. Someone to protect. And damned if he wasn't still thinking of Chris that way, even now that he was lost. Dylan felt one of the knots in his chest loosen a little: Chris might hate him now, but at least Chris would be safe.

"Got a little news," Rick said after a long silence.

"Yeah?"

"Turns out my little wigglers are alive and well, and one of them was a brave little soldier."

It took Dylan a moment to decipher this, but when he did he whooped with joy, jumped from his seat, and ran around the table to give his brother a hug. "Ow," Dylan said, pulling away. "I think physical stuff is a little premature for me."

"Then I'll skip the ass kicking you deserve for being so goddamn stubborn."

Dylan punched Rick on the shoulder. "When's she due?"

"January fifteenth." Rick was grinning from ear to ear.

"Are you happy or scared shitless?"

"Um… about fifty-fifty, but the ratio shifts."

"You guys will be the best parents ever."

Rick smiled at him. "And you'll be Uncle Dyldo."

ALTHOUGH Chris had apparently taken some pains to hide the burial site, Dylan had little trouble finding it. Maybe most people wouldn't have noticed, but his hunter's eyes knew the look of recently disturbed ground, and he could still smell fresh earth. Chris had chosen a spot in the middle of the Christmas trees, in between a large downed limb and a clump of young sumacs. Dylan had to scramble over a fair amount of debris to get there, but he didn't even feel a twinge anymore. Supernatural healing was an amazing thing.

He stood over the makeshift grave and thought about whether he should clear the area a little, maybe make a small stone cairn. He wasn't sorry for what he'd done—he'd do it again to save Chris or Rick or Kay—and he wasn't sure there had been any way for him to avoid the situation. Even if he'd told Chris what he was, Andy still would have come around and might very well have attacked Chris out of jealousy or spite or some misguided attempt to win Dylan back. And to be honest, Dylan was relieved to know that Andy wouldn't be haunting him anymore.

But he was still a little sad. He could understand Andy's desperation to have someone to call his own, someone to love him. Yes, his way of trying to get those things was pretty fucked up, but then Dylan wasn't exactly the healthy-relationship poster boy himself. Maybe once upon a time Andy had been a decent guy, a normal person with a job and friends and a home. Maybe he used to like to watch football on Sundays and do crosswords and spend long weekends at the coast. Dylan didn't really know much at all about Andy, apart from how he liked to fuck—and that was sad too.

"I hope you're running happily somewhere," Dylan said quietly. "Good hunting, Andy."

An early season heat wave had settled in, and as Dylan headed back to the house he felt sticky. He was going to take a cool shower but then realized he had his own private swimming hole, so he turned instead down the pathway toward the pond. He was going to have to rent a Cat or something soon; the brambles were starting to really take over.

The ducks were back, eyeing him disapprovingly from the opposite end of the pond as he stripped off his sweaty clothes. "Don't worry," he told them. "I'm not in the mood for foie gras today." They quacked a response.

The water was cold enough to make him yelp, and the mud squished between his toes. He waded out until the water was shoulder deep, then submerged himself. He came up sputtering and spitting, already nicely chilled. He wasn't much of a swimmer, but he rolled onto his back and floated there for a while, gazing up at a robin's egg sky edged with a thousand shades of green. He'd never swum naked before. It was kind of freeing.

He was still drifting on the water when he heard the growl of an engine. At first he assumed the farmer who rented Chris's land was plowing or something—Dylan was still pretty vague about the specifics of farming activity. But then he realized that the sound was much too close for that, and coming closer. Alarmed, he splashed his way back to shore. Between the water on his skin and the mud on his feet and the tightness of his jeans, it was quickly apparent that getting his pants back on without falling on his ass was going to be an impossibility. "Fuck it. My farm," he muttered and wrapped his shirt around his waist as a sort of makeshift loincloth. He toed his sandals back on and trotted up the hill.

And nearly got run over by a small tractor.

As Dylan hopped out of the way—getting himself good and scratched by the blackberries in the process—the Cat came to a shuddering halt. "Dig the outfit," Chris said with a half smile.

"What the hell?"

"Told you this needed clearing. By the time you figure out how to do it, the bramble's gonna be big enough to fight back."

"But... but...."

"Could use some cash. You still got your job, right?"

Dylan tried to make his tongue work. "Uh, yeah. Sure."

"Good." Chris reached as if to turn the machine back on.

"Wait!" Dylan cried. "I thought—you said you wanted me out of your life."

Chris was silent a moment, and then he shrugged. "Kinda hard to do when you live next door. Kept picturin' you like old Uncle Frank, glarin' at me from that window."

"I didn't... I wasn't—"

"Didn't say you were. Just said I was picturin' it."

Dylan felt ridiculous standing mostly naked among the thorns while having this conversation. A jay squawked from a nearby tree, as if it were laughing at him. Dylan tilted his head and squinted to get a better look into the cab. "Does this mean you'll help me with the reno too?"

"Yeah, I guess."

"It doesn't bother you to work with a werewolf?"

Chris gave him a long look and then hopped out of the Cat. Little trickles of sweat had formed around his hairline and were sliding down his tan neck. Dylan licked his lips and then had to look away.

"Dude, I didn't care that you were a pretentious latte-swilling hipster wannabe with a goddamn Prius and NPR coffee cups and irony oozing from your pores. I can live with fuckin' Fido once a month. Enough to work with you, anyway."

Dylan struggled to bring his heart rate under control. He wondered whether werewolves could have cardiac arrests. "But you were so angry at me."

"You think that's 'cause you're a wolf?"

"Well... yeah. And because I almost got you killed."

"Asshole." Chris folded his arms across his chest. He gave a pointed look at the scars on Dylan's torso. "You fuckin' bounced in there like a comic book hero and wiped the floor with that bastard. I didn't get a scratch on me, and you got your guts scooped out. I ain't mad at you over that."

"Then… what?" Dylan shook his head in confusion.

Chris pointed angrily at him, his finger like a weapon. "You didn't fuckin' trust me! I let you see… let you see what I am, but you couldn't fuckin' let the stupid hick know what you are."

"You're far from stupid, Chris."

"Goddamn it!" Chris pounded the tractor behind him so hard that Dylan wondered if he'd dented the metal. "You stand there and act like you fuckin' respect me, like you think I'm… I'm worthy of you. But you think I can't handle reality, that I'm gonna scream like a little girl, like fuckin' Little Red Riding Hood."

Dylan took a step closer, almost within reach. "That wasn't it."

"Then you thought I'd sell your story to… to the *National Enquirer* or *Fox News* or some other goddamn idiots."

"Honestly, that never even occurred to me," Dylan replied.

"Then why didn't you trust me?" shouted Chris.

Dylan's answer was almost a whisper. "I knew you'd leave me when you found out. I was… trying to delay the inevitable, I guess. Hoarding my time with you."

A strange look came over Chris's face. "You didn't trust me to love you."

Dylan had never before wanted to laugh and cry at the same time. "Why would you?"

"Oh, dude." Chris closed the space between them and gathered Dylan into his arms. His hands were hot and rough on Dylan's bare skin, his hair was dusty and full of bits of leaves and twigs, and he smelled strongly of sweat and tobacco smoke. Dylan closed his eyes, inhaled, and allowed some of his weight to rest against Chris. His fingers clutched at the soft cotton of Chris's T-shirt. "You're such a fuckin' moron," Chris said against his shoulder.

The kiss that followed wasn't the longest or hottest or most toe-curling they'd ever shared. Chris tasted like cigarettes and onions, and Dylan was in imminent danger of losing his loincloth altogether. But it was the most wonderful kiss Dylan had ever had, and all the knots in his chest finally unraveled, allowing him to breathe freely for the first time in years.

"Is this going to be okay?" he asked when they pulled slightly apart. "You and me, I mean."

Chris seemed to consider the question. "We're gonna need a little work, maybe." He laughed slightly. "We're both kind of a mess."

Dylan glanced over Chris's shoulder, where the back of his house was visible. Paint peeling, windows uncurtained, no mud room even begun yet. But still beautiful in its own way. Good bones, and full of potential.

"Yeah," Dylan said. "We need some renovations. But I think we've got a good foundation, and our structure is sound."

Chris smiled at him. Not a half grin, but a full and toothy smile that crinkled his eyes and made him look like a delighted teenager. "All right then, Dyl. Let's get to work."

ACKNOWLEDGMENTS

Many people think of writing as a solitary activity, but *Good Bones* would never have come to fruition without contributions from several wonderful people. Karen Witzke's careful and thoughtful feedback was invaluable, but not as invaluable as her friendship. I'd also like to thank Sheree Adams, who was willing to look at my manuscript (quickly!) and who gave me the confidence to believe that my story was one that people would want to read. Amy Lane read my first (self-published) novel and suggested I consider submitting to Dreamspinner Press; her encouragement was exactly the spark I needed. Finally, I am deeply grateful to my amazingly supportive husband, who gives me the space and time I need to write, and who's proud to tell people he's married to an author.

KIM FIELDING is very pleased every time someone calls her eclectic. She has migrated back and forth across the western two-thirds of the United States and currently lives in California, where she long ago ran out of bookshelf space. She's a university professor who dreams of being able to travel and write full-time. She also dreams of having two perfectly behaved children, a husband who isn't obsessed with football, and a house that cleans itself. Some dreams are more easily obtained than others.

Kim can be found on her blogs: http://kfieldingwrites.blogspot.com/ and http://www.goodreads.com/author/show/4105707.Kim_Fielding/ blog and on Facebook: http://www.facebook.com/#!/pages/ Kim-Fielding/286938444652579. Her e-mail is dephalqu@yahoo.com.

Read more by KIM FIELDING in

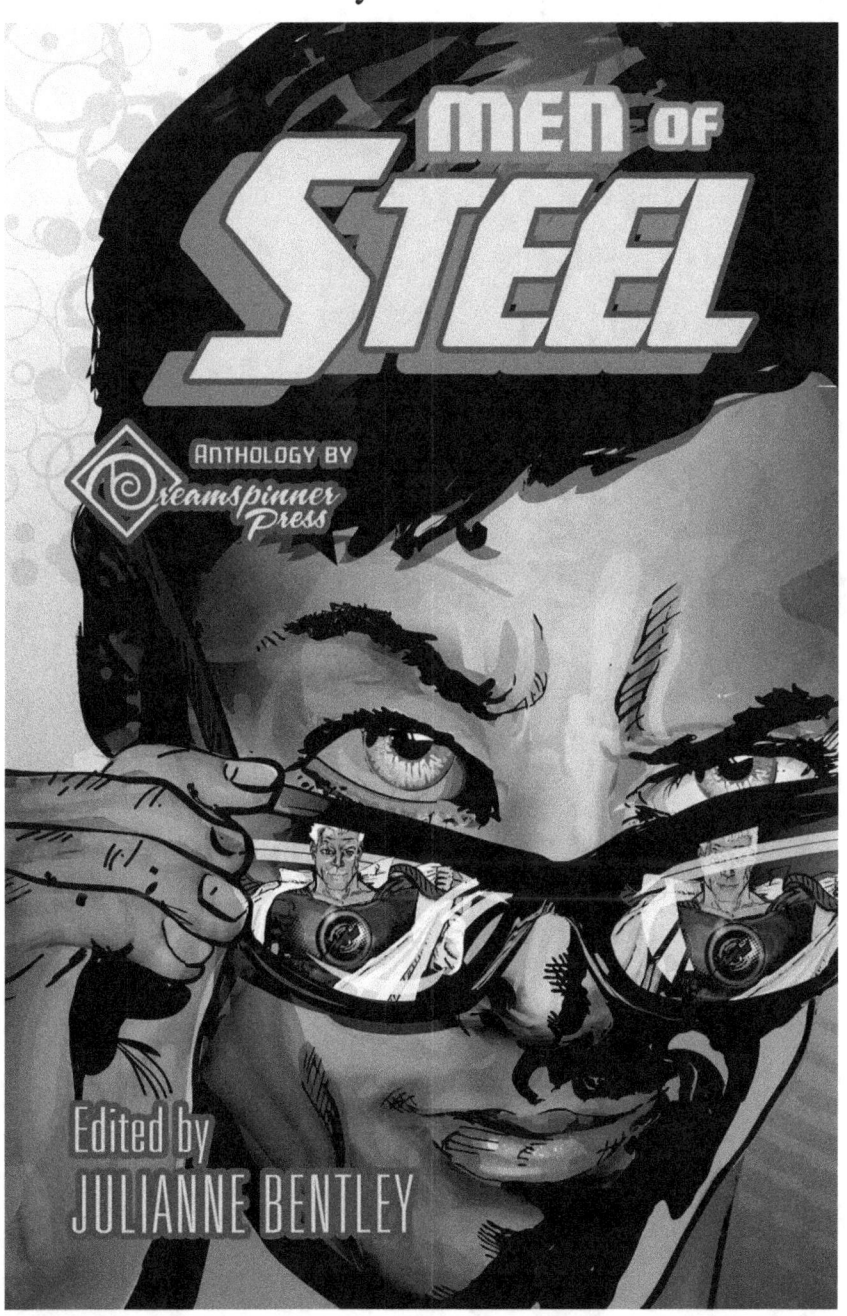

Paranormal Romance from DREAMSPINNER PRESS

www.ingramcontent.com/pod-product-compliance
Lightning Source LLC
Chambersburg PA
CBHW070017260626
47159CB00005B/1847